"Fly with Me This Night on Wild Wings of Love . . ."

The poetry of Bron's words filled Eithne, but she could speak none of her own aloud. She reached for him, clasping his thick hair in her fists, and drew his face up to her own. In the starlight she could see the flash of his teeth as he smiled.

A wild heat fired her blood and she became bold and kissed him as he kissed her—meeting his tongue, moving her lips against his.

"Sweet witch!" he groaned. Their union was like a dawning daylight rainbow carrying them upward into deep wonder . . . downward into silent pools of crystalline communion.

Her soul bursting, she met his emerald gaze. *I love you. I have always loved you.*

"You love because you are loved. You have enchanted me without enchantment, my swan witch."

'Tis only the beginning . . .

Books by Betina Lindsey

The Serpent Beguiled
Swan Bride
Swan Witch
Waltz with the Lady

Published by POCKET BOOKS

SWAN WITCH

BETINA LINDSEY

POCKET BOOKS

New York   London   Toronto   Sydney   Tokyo   Singapore

This book is a work of fiction. Names, characters, places, and incidents either are products of the author's imagination or are used fictitiously. Any resemblance to actual events or locales or persons, living or dead, is entirely coincidental.

An *Original* Publication of POCKET BOOKS

POCKET BOOKS, a division of Simon & Schuster Inc.
1230 Avenue of the Americas, New York, NY 10020

ISBN: 0-671-75171-9

First Pocket Books printing November 1993

10 9 8 7 6 5 4 3 2 1

POCKET and colophon are registered trademarks of Simon & Schuster Inc.

Cover art by Aleta Jenks

Printed in the U.S.A.

For my children, Eowyn, Tessa, Stryder, Ethan, and Shae, that they may keep their hearts open and learn to love more than to fear.

A special thanks to Stryder for his expertise in all things magick . . . and to James, a wise soul, and to my parents, Jess and Wanda.

Let those love now who never loved;
  Let those who have loved love again . . .
                    —*Coventry Patmore*

SWAN WITCH

Chapter

In the season of rains, when the rivers of Banba roar past the rocks along their banks and winter-dead leaves swirl away in the rush of sun-lit water, a solitary warrior by the name of Bron mac Llyr traveled westward. His sword arm hung limp at his side wrapped in a swaddling of linen. With but a stump for a hand, he rode to the inner kingdoms in search of the legendary swan sister, Ketha, the only healer in Banba who might restore it.

The stain of dried blood darkened the gold and silver running border of his sky blue cloak. His long raven hair was braided like that of a king and his emerald eyes held the knowing of the Tuatha de Danann, the people of the goddess Danu.

Attached to the leathers of his saddle was a shield, dented by the blows of battle and emblazoned with a dolphin leaping the crest of an ocean wave. A harp hung beside the shield. Before the battle at Carrowmore there were few in the Western Isles who would not traverse a league to hear the harper Bron mac Llyr. Now few walked across their own threshold to exchange a common greeting.

The late afternoon was peaceful enough as he broke from the forest of oak and ash. Ahead rose the circular rath of an ancient stronghold. He had not expected it. He drew up his steed, hesitant to ride into the queer ground mist that seemed to foment from the rath's moat. The stench of rotting flesh wafted on the breeze. Bron constricted his nostrils and began to breathe through his mouth. His great war-horse, Samisen, snorted, no stranger to the smells of death and battle.

With his good hand, Bron stroked the horse gently and with a canny eye surveyed the stronghold's expanse from flagged towers to dry-stone cashels.

In a low tone he spoke to Samisen. "'Tis a prosperous but dark abode. I would give you your head, but I have no inclination to charge into the unknown. Then again what have we to lose? We have wandered a fortnight in these strange lands without cross-pathing a living soul."

Cautiously, he nudged his destrier forward, hearing only the sigh of the wind in the trees and the creaking of his saddle. As he approached the bridge, he reined in, for along the railings like so many apples were piked the decaying heads of men. Ten on first count.

"Mayhap we have arrived at the kingdom of the dead," he said as a crook-necked scavenger took wing.

He swallowed back his distaste, and in a natural reflex the swaddled nub of his arm moved to rest on the hilt of his sword. He winced with the anger and frustration of his own impotency. A moon month had passed since his defeat in the battle of Carrowmore. The wrist wound festered as brightly as the vivid memory of the Fomorian chieftain slicing off his hand. Many times since he'd wished the Fomorian had killed him outright, for a warrior and a harper was better dead than handless.

A bird's *whilloo* from the battlement walk above caused him to look up. He spied no bird, but the slender form of a flame tressed maiden. Her face was in shadow, but the crimson light of the setting sun haloed her hair and figure as if it were afire with netherworld witchery.

She leaned dangerously over the parapet; never had he seen such a look of deterrence on so beauteous a face.

Be gone! See your fate! Her mouth did not move nor did a sound pass her lips, but like the unseen wind he was as sure as earth the warning came from the maid.

Who was she? As Bron stared at her, she met his gaze full force. For the first time in many months, he felt an emotion stirring in him that was not despondence.

In the same instant a guard bellowed from the barbican. "A welcome to you, traveler. I'll raise the gate."

In the wavering sunlight, Bron pulled his eyes from the maiden to the guard and back again.

She had disappeared.

The screak of iron groaned in the air. Bron's eyes narrowed. Intrigued, he was not so great a fool to rush in.

"Cross now or never. I have more to do with my day than await your knightly pleasure. My supper grows cold."

Still Bron kept his seat, his eyes giving the dry-stone cashels one more swift scan.

"Be you named Coward Heart?" came the guard's impatient challenge.

Bron grinned at the insult though his warrior's sense shouted that something was amiss here. Still, the mention of supper shifted his wariness. "Nay, friend. I am called Bron, Bron the hungry."

The guard laughed. "Enter and be fed, Bron the hungry."

Enter and be decapitated, thought Bron more circumspectly. He readily saw that the stronghold gate so quickly lifted to the lone traveler could serve the dual purpose of imprisoning him inside. "May I ask the name of this stronghold and the name of the lord at whose table I might sit?"

"You can. 'Tis Rath Morna, the abode of Sheelin the Druid." Bron searched his memory but had not heard of this place or this druid, Sheelin. But then he was not so familiar with the inner kingdoms of Banba for his roots were among the off land isles of the sea. He whispered to his steed, "The choice is yours, Samisen. I'll rely upon your creature instincts as always. If fortune turns, must needs be we will fly out."

The stallion shook its cascading white mane, shuffled backward as its great silver shod hooves thumped indecision on the wood planked bridge. Then, with a confident snort, he arched his head and tail nobly. He

4

trotted forward past the grotesque and gaping heads, beneath the sharp-fanged portcullis and into the stronghold's center yard.

Not a second after Samisen's flowing tail passed, like a rattrap in a peasant's prison, the portcullis garroted shut. Bron did not look to his back, but composed his features with boldness and faced all watchers gallantly. Indeed, the smithy held his hammer midstrike, the candle maker's tallow solidified in his ladle, and the children ceased their game of kick gut. Except for the sleeping babes in their mother's arms every gaze within the stronghold branded him.

He slipped back the hood of his cloak and announced with a deferring nod, "I am Bron mac Llyr."

"Greetings! Bron mac Llyr," came a commanding, deep voice. Bron's gaze lifted to a high casement of the keep. "I am Sheelin of Rath Morna."

Despite his shocking white hair, Sheelin's bold-featured face held not a wrinkle of age nor was his pleasant greeting marked in his dark eyes. Bron tightened his lips and inwardly weighed the wisdom of entering the gates of a man whose smile did not reach above his mouth.

"Honor to you, Sheelin of Rath Morna," deferred Bron, bowing his head and touching his breast.

At that moment a young servant girl ran down the keep's steps with a bouquet of bittersweet and white roses. After a short curtsy on tiptoe she presented the flowers to Bron, which he took in his good hand.

"We are in need of new diversion at Rath Morna. My castle is yours, Bron mac Llyr. Let it never be said I am an ungenerous host. Stable his horse, Coup,"

Sheelin ordered, his voice echoing clearly in the stiff silence of the center yard. "Enter, and be welcomed."

The druid's silk capped head disappeared within the keep. The gateman hastened forward and reached for Samisen's gold bridle.

Still silent, all watched Bron mac Llyr. The servant girl swatted at flies, but mainly like everyone else she waited to see what he might do. Bron rubbed the stubble of his beard consideringly. Then he spoke to the gateman. "First, I will see to my mount myself."

"As you please, milord." Coup stepped back affably.

Bron slipped down off Samisen and without need of lead reins the horse followed him as he in turn followed the gateman. "So you are called Coup."

"Aye, Coup de Grace."

Bron smiled, then sobered. "Then 'tis your handiwork I saw displayed on the bridge pikes."

"'Tis."

"What was their crime?"

"The crime of folly."

"Do not all men share in this crime? Why then is folly punishable by death at Rath Morna?"

"You have not heard about the proclamation?"

"Nay, I am a stranger to these lands."

"Hah and ha-ha!" Laughter shook his barrel chest. "Our friendship shall be short. 'Tis too late for you. You enter our gates more the fool of folly than the poor devils who greeted you on the bridge."

"Pray, can you not make a fool like myself the wiser, before you sever my neck and chin?"

"I might, then I might not. What profit to me if I make you the wiser?"

"If you think to inherit my fine destrier upon my death, think again. 'Tis Sheelin the Druid who will take possession of so rare a beast." Bron knew anyone with two eyes might see that Samisen was a faerie horse of the Tuatha de Danann. He was a rare breed of horse—fleet as the wind, with the arched neck and the broad chest and the quivering nostrils, and the large eyes that showed he was made of fire and flame, and not of dull heavy earth.

Coup scratched his bearded jaw. "Aye, you speak true. Be sure, I am not greedy, but a man does what he must to earn his way. What else have you to barter for a bit of information?"

"Naught, for as you see my sword hand is severed."

"What of this harp?"

"Mayhap I can play you half a song . . . but only half, friend. If oft time you go a courting I can teach you a song which will win a maiden's love."

"I have no voice for it."

"You need not sing. Merely spoken, the verse will melt even the coldest maiden's heart."

"Truth?"

"Truth!"

"There is a woman. . . . She will not have me near her. She says I stink of death. But I have been thinking of retirement and would fancy being tended in my old age. By dung! 'Tis a trade—my words for yours."

"Then speak, man, if my life is short I'll not waste the moment more. Tell me of this proclamation."

"Sheelin has a daughter. Eithne is as clever a witch as she is beautiful—and that is saying a great amount for she is one of the fairest who has walked the earth. He has proclaimed that any man who can answer in truth a question Eithne will ask, and will ask a question she can in truth answer, should have her for his bride along with treasures beyond imaginings."

"That does not seem so difficult."

"Not to the fool of folly. But, my foolish friend, Eithne is mute. She does not speak."

"I see." Now it was Bron who scratched his chin. "Is it too late to turn back?" he asked, challenged by this paradox.

"For a knight like yourself, once you crossed that bridge, the only way out of Rath Morna is the chopping axe."

"So I must make the mute maiden speak if I am to live."

"Take heart," said Coup as he slapped Bron good-naturedly on the shoulder. "For seven days and seven nights you will live as a king. All at Rath Morna will be at your disposal."

"And then . . ."

A compassionate twinkle lit Coup's dark eyes. "For a friend, I will hone my axe mercifully sharp!"

Her teeth clenched with rage, Eithne peered over the stone wall and glared down at the stranger in the center yard. Would it never stop? How many more heads would roll at her feet before this nightmare ended?

Tears stung her eyes. Her slim fingers dug into the

stone and her knuckles whitened. No matter the consequence, prince and peasant, vagabond and tramp one by one still came to Rath Morna to cross the "bridge of buzzards" for that is what it was called now. What kept them coming? None loved her. None even knew her. The promise of riches then? Nay, her father lied. He would never part with a tittle of his great wealth nor let her loose from his sorcery—of course the fools did not know this.

She watched while the snowy steed dipped its head proudly and its master rode straight backed with eye-fixing presence. She listened as Sheelin greeted him with all the cunning of a buttery-tongued dragon to his lair. She cried silent tears as the raven haired knight bent to take the proffered bouquet from the gentle child, Gilly.

Would the man ever come who could match Sheelin? The one man who was different, the way gold is from bronze, or diamonds from glass shards? She picked out details—the fall of his fine black hair over tarnished chest armor. The neatly swathed hand and darned leggings. He appeared cleanly, at least. Her probing gaze moved to the ornately carved harp hanging against the horse's well-groomed white coat. He must have a talent, she decided.

Aye, it had all happened before. She'd met each suitor with fierce resistance. Resourcefully, she'd single-handedly thwarted their advances. But it was always the same ending, one which haunted her dreams and tormented her waking hours.

She could watch no more! She turned away, feeling as if she were drowning in his blood already. Whoever he was, he needed no more misfortune in his life. Why had he not heeded her warning?

Down the tower stairs she stumbled, down through a door which opened into a maze of foundation passages. At last she reached the drain tunnel to the outer walls. On hands and knees she crawled through the dark channel and along the vine overgrown bank beneath the arched shelter of the bridge. Her heart bursting with misery she coiled her arms around her knees and rocked to and fro.

"Begobs, gurrul, pwhat ye twitching about?" gargled a small voice. A gangling body emerged fully from an oozing sinkhole at the moat's edge.

Eithne lifted her head and attempted to wipe her tear sodden face but only succeeded in smearing mud moss over her cheeks. As was her gift to use when she chose, she opened her thoughts to him. *Beway, Gibbers, I can't bear it!*

"Pwhat is beyant bearing?"

Her wretched eyes looked into his own boggish grimace.

More than you, a swamp beast, will ever know.

The translucent skin of his second eyelid glazed his gob green orbs and his lipless mouth cracked wide with morbidity. His pointed ears twitched and his skinny limbs curled around his distended belly with cloying interest.

"Begorrah, another divil's a cumm!" He chuckled with an ogre's delight. "It's beyant my understandin'. They be all fools a wantin' wan woman whin the worruld is full o' thim. Tell me yer throubles, gurrul. I like to hear thim."

Indeed you do. 'Tis not your scaled body their grasping hands paw with lust. 'Tis not your throat they choke in shaking you to speech. Nor is it your eyes they implore or your face they last see at the chopping block.

"Thrue, but I wish it were." He grinned salaciously.

You little demon. You feed upon my misery like a perverted green glutton and then you gossip about the countryside to any snail or slug who passes.

"Don't be shh . . . notty," he sniveled. "Fer sartain no other cares a twat about you. Who else will hear yer throubles as I. Who else? Whoooo? Whooooooo?" he taunted, and flapped his stringy arms.

No one, thought Eithne with heart dragging resignation. Since childhood, when her mother disappeared, she'd always come beneath the bridge to Gibbers. He might be spiteful, cold-blooded, and a gross gossip, but he was there.

"Blathers . . . shpeak to me of this vagabone. The weight of his shtallion shook the boards of my bridge."

'Tis no wonder for it is an uncommonly great beast and he sits upon its back with more arrogance than all the others put together. By gesture and voice he is highborn, but not highborn enough for me.

"Musha, the Dagda himself would not be highborn enough fer ye. But I care not. Pwhat of his nilly noggin? How will his head beset my bridge?"

Mayhap this one is too handsome for your bridge.

"He's not redheaded, is hee? Presarve us from babby faced redheads."

He's neither, you bog child. He wears his raven locks in the long braids of a prince and warrior. He's tall, with eyes as sharp as a Drusheen raptor and shoulders wide enough to turn the hearts o' half the women in Banba. He is called Bron mac Llyr and bears the emblems of a sea isle clan. Eithne surprised even herself with her vehemence in praising him.

"Will you be shweet with him this night?" he asked, leering. "Or make him dance with brimstone as you av' the others?"

You needn't speculate. I will do what I must do. He'll be no exception. The moat mist licked her toes and for a moment she yearned to be as the mist, without form, without mind, without heart. If only it could be different this one time.

"Be sartain, in the end Sheelin will grab yer voice and the seycrets of yer powers. Yer mother cud not win against him nor cun ye."

Soon, I'll discover where he has imprisoned my mother and together we will flee to Myr.

"Niver be so foolish to think he'll not follow ye with his legions of demons and magics. Ye'll nade a clan of warriors at yer back the likes of yer fair-faced fool on his great beastie."

That one has seen battle enough, he is already missing a hand.

"No hand? Och, he who has no hand will soon have no head."

She glared at him. *Do not speak so.*

"Indade, I'll shpeak as I plase. Bekase of ye, he'll loose his head. Yer a wicked, evil gurrul."

She lowered her eyes and turned away. *We are all evil at Rath Morna.*

Chapter

Torches blazed bright and golden goblets brimmed with crimson wine. Servants carried tankards and trays of choice delicacies, garnished roasted game to overladen feast tables. Richly dressed minstrels played leaping melodies for the dancing knights and bejeweled ladies of Sheelin's court.

There was no one as hungry as Bron mac Llyr. While beckoning to each and every servant who passed, he filled his plate with baked quail and steamed fish, cheese and bread, honeyed berries and plump cream pastries. Not even in the high king's court had he experienced such splendor.

A thought niggled in his mind and caused him to pause midchew. Aye, there was a sense of excess and decadence within the walls of Rath Morna. Though wellborn, he'd been raised to live simply, that others might simply live. In his travels he'd waylaid in high courts and lowly hovels, feasting with king and supping with cottager, but never had he witnessed such a flaunting extravagance.

13

As if reading his mind, Sheelin asked in a prideful voice from his high seat, "Tell me, Bron mac Llyr, have you ever seen the likes of this in your travels?"

Bron turned to the black-eyed druid and answered truthfully, "I have not."

In that moment a drunken Fir Darrig jumped upon the table and leered into Bron's face. His wizened body was incongruous with his fancy attire. Whiskery rat ears pointed out from beneath his tall hat and a hairy rat tail curled from beneath his red velvet coat. In truth, his grotesque appearance was an oddity amidst the elegant court. He snatched a meaty bone from a platter and retreated to sit on the arm of Sheelin's great throne.

Sheelin's lip curled in a sneer. He gave the Fir Darrig a hard slap. It tumbled to the floor and scrambled under the banquet table with his bone. Bron knew that Fir Darrigs delighted in treachery of a rather gruesome nature. He fought the impulse to look under the table to see what the creature was about.

"What brings you to the inner realms? Your crest marks you as a sea clansman," Sheelin queried forthrightly.

"I am seeking someone," began Bron honestly, lifting his gaze from beneath the table.

"And who do you seek?"

"As you see I have but one hand."

"Yes . . ."

"I am seeking a healer, the swan sister Ketha. I believe she is the sole healer in Banba who might restore my hand." From under the table came a shrill cackle.

Sheelin's complacency shifted into affront. The laughter and talk of those surrounding them ceased and a tense silence held the air. All eyes watched Sheelin. His dark eyes narrowed. Bron felt the mire of that darkness like a cloud hanging in the hall.

"I know no one by that name," Sheelin announced too loudly.

Along the benches Bron saw many exchange uneasy glances and he suspected here at Rath Morna much was hidden. If Sheelin did not know of Ketha, others did.

"If missing a hand is all that keeps you from enjoying yourself, observe . . ."

His fingers fanned the air over Bron's arm. Suddenly before his very eyes, Bron's hand was restored.

After the first shock of pleasure, he lifted his arm and exercised his fingers with a tentative skepticism. The appearance of a whole hand was before him. Yet, he felt no sense of touch or strength in his fingers. He looked back at Sheelin.

"This swan witch is not the only one who might heal your hand," said Sheelin, arrogance strolling over his features. "Now enjoy yourself. Eat, be merry." He stood and waved his arms through the air and the hall fairly dazzled with abundance and luxury.

Suspicion whirling in his mind, Bron closed his eyes and whispered beneath his breath, "If this be illusion, veil fall."

He blinked, opened his eyes, and for a brief second he saw the court of Rath Morna for what it was. The delicacies on his plate were not rare sweetmeats but maggots and slugs. The silken tapestries draping the walls were ragged shreds and the bouquets of flowers bedecking the hall, dried weeds. The angelic-faced servants were wretched beasts enslaved by sorcery and beneath all the sweet fragrances the odor of swamp stench stung his nose. The dancers who swayed and shimmied before him still smiled, but with the visages of blood-sucking kelpies.

Lastly, he looked at his hand and saw it too was an illusion. He was not immune to the disappointment and felt resentment toward Sheelin for his deception. He realized he sat within an Unseelie Court of weird and conjured monstrosities.

There was great power at Rath Morna and his glimpse beneath the illusion was brief. When he blinked again, the illusion returned more vividly than before.

In front of him, what seconds ago had been rabbit dung and rotted fruit, now became plump pears and sugared grapes overflowing a silver platter. With his hand, he reached and attempted to clutch a goblet. His fingers passed through the stem. He swallowed with distaste. With his functional hand he pushed aside his plate, his appetite wholly diminished.

"I see my powers have left you at a loss for words, Bron mac Llyr," said Sheelin with expectancy.

Bron near laughed aloud, but he schooled his features with reserve.

"You need not thank me," continued Sheelin.

"'Tis a common enough feat. Now eat your fill!" he commanded, lounging back in his high seat. He began to laugh heartily. "There is more where this came from."

"Indeed, I believe you." Bron frowned, his emerald eyes smoldering with the knowing of Sheelin's ruse. He himself was no stranger to such sorcery being the son of the sorcerer sea king, Manannan mac Llyr, who held the power of invisibility and seeing through the illusion of others who were.

However, Bron had no inclination for the sorcerer's avocation and resented its misuse. Dung dressed in illusion and dipped in honey was still dung no matter how grandiose the gala.

Sheelin leaned toward him. "If whatever you want is not here, merely ask and I will personally see to it."

Bron tipped his head politely and spoke, "My thanks, your graciousness. Your table is beyond belief, but I have feasted enough. My stomach swells and my appetite cowers in the face of another bite." He reached for a quill toothpick and waved off an approaching servant.

"No matter." Sheelin smiled as he pushed away from the table and came to his feet. "Your dessert comes."

At that moment a maiden stepped into the hall and Bron turned his gaze to her. She was lily fair, with masses of red-gold hair, her figure truly lovely with seraphic breasts and round hips. Slender and fine, she moved flowingly like the sea. Was she a sorceress? Like an exotic wildcat's, her wide eyes mesmerized him. He stared, recognizing her to be the woman who had given him the warning not to enter Rath Morna.

"Eithne, you are late!" Sheelin chastened sharply. "Come sit! Sit beside your suitor."

Gowned in clouds of dragonfly silks, she fairly floated through the hall and dipped an indifferent curtsy before her glaring father, taking the seat opposite from where he'd directed.

She fully faced Bron mac Llyr. Before he'd not seen her in good light. He saw that her eyes were an intricate mosaic of swirling color. For a split second she leveled the full magnificent potency of them upon him. Then, as he sat there feeling as if he'd just been given divine audience, she shuttered her eyes and looked through him as if he were a pillar holding up the hall.

Again, he tried to catch her eye. She would not have it. Her rowan lips were tomb tight and her brow arched to haughtiness.

She was a beauty to be sure, though from experience Bron had learned the greater the beauty, the greater the artifice. He toyed with what she might really look like beneath her father's finely crafted illusion. Mayhap she was a merrow hag or grizzly Grendel. He saw himself lying in her hairy arms, her single long nailed claw stroking his perspiring forehead.

Now the wiser, he raised his false hand to cover the emerging mirth which curved his lips. For the moment he had no inclination to spoil the illusion and chose to rub along with the night's sorcery. He had no fear of it. Conjured monsters were the playmates of his youth, each and every had been a loving gift from his father to school away his fears, test his strength, and awaken his compassion. Yet, he'd never gone so far as to bed one.

"Might I have the attention of one and all." Sheelin clapped. The minstrels paused midsong and the hall settled with an air of anticipation.

Bron's eyes remained on Eithne while hers swirled with glazed detachment. Though he'd been studying her a goodly time, he was not sure of their color. The dark and lights of her pupils shifted like opal rainbows.

"'Tis the time to acquaint my fair Eithne with her suitor, Bron mac Llyr. From the depths of my heart I hope she will him with good grace and geniality." He turned to Bron and said with apology, "Never was a maid so winsome, yet unwilling as my Eithne. Your task is to make her winsome as well as willing."

An odd, vulgar chuckle rippled through the hall.

"You've seven days and seven nights to answer in truth a question Eithne will ask, and ask a question she can in truth answer," Sheelin continued on. "By the end of seven days, Bron mac Llyr, you will have all or nothing. I call a toast for a favorable outcome." He raised a golden goblet high. "All hail! Long life to Bron mac Llyr!"

"Long life," echoed those in the hall.

Bron came to his feet and took his cup in hand. "All hail!" he summoned. He bowed gallantly to Eithne and said, "My cup I lift to a lady fair, beautiful and comely. My voice I raise in selfish plea, a flowing tongue to Lady Eithne!"

Laughter shook the air but none spilled across the lips of Eithne. Bron saw her demeanor was as taut as a hunter's bow and her gaze a thousand arrows aimed solely at him. Well, he thought bemused, I have at least caught her attention once more.

As all others drank the toast, she suddenly took a goblet in her delicate hand. She lifted it, not to her lips, but poured its contents in a spreading pool on the table before Bron. Her insult was clear . . . her intent not to speak even clearer.

This intrigued him for he had not thought an illusion could mimic such independent behavior, unless perhaps she was no dressed up ghoul.

"Eithne!" came a black warning from Sheelin. She did not turn eye or head to him. Bron saw the heavy flush of temper cross his face as he muttered, "You hag spawn, do not pretend you do not hear me! All know you hear as well as speak." Then he hissed under his breath. "'Tis your stubborn neck I should set on the chopping block."

With ill ease, Bron witnessed not a father's impatient reprimand, but a thrust of pure malevolence. Aye, he'd suspected she could speak, but why at the cost of so many lives did she choose not to? The mystery of Rath Morna deepened.

He quickly set aside his cup and rose to his feet, inserting himself between her and her father. Bowing, he requested, "My lady, Eithne, will you dance with me?"

Ignoring him, she kept her eyes lowered.

"Eithne," came the sharp spearing nudge of Sheelin's voice. "You will dance with him."

Surprisingly, she nodded an acceptance as if she could no longer tolerate her father's proximity. Lifting her chimera of skirts she stood and Bron followed her lead to the dancers' circle.

Since the battle of Carrowmore he had shunned women. A maimed warrior did not pay court to wellborn ladies. Now, in the illusion he could. He presented his sword hand. Within his heart he wished it were not an illusion and she as fair as she appeared. With a pause of hesitation, her own slim fingers reached for the illusion.

Her fingers clasped thin air.

In the moment of awkwardness, her eyes softened from the angry hues of marsh fire to a sympathetic magenta. The last thing he wanted was her sympathy. Yet, he'd been the fool who for a short moment had unwittingly believed the illusion. No, he amended, he'd not believed it . . . he'd wanted to believe it. There was a difference.

He offered his other hand instead. She took his palm. He felt her warmth and substance. But was that real, he wondered? Still, in this moment he'd no desire to expose the illusion.

Adroitly, his mind and muscles began to move with the rhythms of the courting dance. In the slow grace of the steps his eyes followed her bows, her crossings and curtsies. When she lifted her skirts for toe pointings he was relieved to spy a slim, well-turned ankle instead of a kelpie's hairy hoof. He could accept the illusion of his hand, but as he followed her willowy languor and lightness of movement he did not want to believe that her grace, beauty, and animation were illusions as well.

Illusion or no, she aroused him.

As Eithne danced with Bron mac Llyr, she wondered what had transpired before she came into the hall. She assumed her father was at his tricks. She despised him for thinking that it would make any difference to her whether the suitor had one hand or two.

Nevertheless, the sounds of pipe, harp, and drum, the tap of heels, the clap of hands, and the bold grace of Bron mac Llyr filled her flagging heart with life. He was taller than she, with a warrior's broad-shouldered build. His hard thighs were clearly outlined by his snug-fitting leggings and his soft leather boots hugged his firm muscled calves. His fine hewn face belied his large frame. Within features encircled by waist length raven hair, she saw a poet and cavalier.

His imperious emerald eyes caught her at her perusal and she averted her gaze aware of the fierce heat flushing her cheeks. She dutifully clasped his whole hand, a cursory touch that confirmed its form, that traced its hard, callused skin. She wondered, could this hand be trusted? Would this man be different from all the others?

The dance which had begun slowly, ceremoniously, now shifted. The drum beat out a strange, throbbing, deepening cadence which became intoxicating. Her worries gave way to the power of Mac Llyr's movements, his scent, his touching. Handed by and being handed to him bred a familiarity. He locked his arms around hers and whisked her around the floor as they moved through the sets and spirals to the center kissing ring. She easily followed his step which was low gliding and well marked. Within the kissing ring a couple teased and entreated and pursued each other by turns.

The music stopped. The couple's lips met.

Eithne stole an apprehensive glance at Mac Llyr. His gaze met hers with a virile glow which shocked through her. Part of her wanted to run from the circle, the other part which was ruled by the night's full moon remained rooted with swimming expectation.

Amidst smothered giggles, the other couple attempted to remain absolutely motionless. Jests poured forth from the revelers around the hall. Reviving the moment, the minstrels struck up again and the dancers leaped into full life. The pair whirled off, leaving the ring.

Eithne was not so adept to sidestep the center ring with Mac Llyr's strong hand about her small waist. Every turn his smile gleamed over white teeth and his bold gaze provoked her sense of vulnerability. Her heart paced, her eyes dipped to the floor, and her mouth felt as dry as desert sand.

The minstrels ceased their playing.

With a gallant step Bron drew near.

Eithne knew she would allow him to kiss her because the estrus fever was upon her. Time after time she had resisted all the others. Wantonly, her look summoned him full force. He would see her wanting in her eyes . . . on the night of full moon she could not disguise it.

In the tense silence of the hall, motionless, she watched his well-set mouth lower to hers. His penetrating gaze smoldered and his lips firmed with self-assurance. Her fingertips, all nerves, lightly balanced against his hard chest. Her breath caught like the lapse of wave as she plunged into the sensation of his kiss. Though his mouth was warm, a shiver rippled through her nearly unlatching her knees. For support, her palms braced against his muscled chest. Everything receded, the laughter, the sporting jests, the sinister court. . . .

For Eithne, nothing existed but the quenching heat of his lips.

Countless full moons she'd walked heath and moorland searching, aching, burning, never knowing for what. Now she knew. She sought *this* kiss. Bron mac Llyr's kiss.

Her lips parted slightly, and his tongue, moist and hot, traced the inner softness of her lips. She opened full mouth, inviting deeper probing. A low chuckle vibrated in his throat. His tongue tip parried with her own and then with an abandoned lustiness he thrust full force into the cavern of her mouth. Eithne trembled with surrender. Suckling him, she tasted and savored his unfamiliar juices.

When the minstrels struck up once again, desire was rising between them like the moon between two arching oaks. As intimate as rustling leaves, their two bodies coursed with the urge to join flesh.

His senses rioting in the endless swell of the moment, Bron would not retreat. Her lips were puffy, swollen, virginal as spring, and her body a sensual promise of pleasurable dark nights to come. Ill fate whetted every entangling second, the hall rang with raucous voices. Still, he lingered because longing was sweet and the awakening erotic current of wild desire running through him even sweeter.

Aye, deep within the voice of reason reminded him she was a conjured visage of Sheelin's sorcery, but in the instance of this kiss he was lost. She became the image of enchantment that he most desired, a beautiful illusion for whom he'd happily die. Before this kiss he'd been no prisoner of Rath Morna, but after . . .

Chapter

A steep spiraling stairway of a hundred steps led from the banquet floor to the high chambers. Eithne lifted her skirts with flourish and dashed upward wishing with all her heart that she had never kissed Bron mac Llyr. But the sea clansman followed, taking the stone steps by twos. He would be the thirteenth to tread behind her to his eventual doom. Her senses churned with regret and something new . . . wanton desire. This one *was* different. Even now, she could not outstrip him upon the stairs as she had the others.

He kept abreast of her. Avoiding his eyes, she stole a sidelong glance at the line of his broad chest. He was not even breathing hard. On her own part it was not exertion alone that set her simple heart pounding.

Reaching the top of the stairs first, he paused and looked to her for direction. She nodded her head left to the blind arcade where molded corbels, decorated with sprigs of roses, arched above the black oak door of her chamber.

He stepped beneath the cove, his long fingers

clasped the door's iron ring latch. He pulled. The loud squawk of aching hinges vibrated through the air.

He chuckled. "You would do well to lard the hinges, milady. Unless," his said, lips curving slightly, "you begrudge your suitors a silent escape."

Eithne frowned. She found no humor in it.

He cleared his throat, full knowing his words missed the mark.

She stepped through the threshold into her chamber. A fire glowed in the hearth casting leaping shadows on barren walls. Fresh rushes cushioned the floor and the pungent aroma of lavender wafted through the air. She crossed the room to the recessed window, climbed upon the stone seat and sat in the pooling rays of moonlight.

She crouched there saying nothing, watching him with feral regard. She must keep her distance from him or her longings would overtake her.

Like the others, he would cross the threshold. The door would swing firmly shut and entrap him with her until dawn. She would serve him with mischief, witchery, and pretense . . . or would she? Aye, this one was different.

He did not cross the threshold, but stood circumspectly before its mouth.

His gaze circled the room measuringly and stopped on her. "Milady, I shall escort you this far. But in no way do I wish to encroach on the privacy of your chambers. I will be content enough to spend this night with my horse, Samisen, in the stables."

His gallantry enchanted her. His restraint stunned her.

Not one of her suitors had ever made such an offer . . . no matter how much she had attempted to maneuver it. Oddly, the one man she burned for, the one suitor her heart accepted . . . declined.

Her eyes wide, she looked at him . . . searchingly. She tried to reconcile her own full-bodied desire for him with the knowledge that in seven days time his handsome face would be a ghoulish mask dressing the bridge of buzzards.

Revulsion waved through her for her part in such darkness. It was right for him to leave her. She deserved no better. Evil tainted her. In weakness she had allowed herself to kiss him knowing full well he could not then resist her. 'Twas an enchanted kiss . . . more evil . . . more magics.

The goddess forgive me, she thought.

No matter how clear-eyed she might appear, no matter how sweetly their two hearts might pass this night, he should not stay.

Yet, it was a full moon and in the light of a full moon no swan maid could deny her longings. And she had chosen him with her kiss.

She gave him a deep soulful gaze. His own emerald eyes were guarded while he postured with courtliness. His earlier susceptibility seemed to have dissolved with the disengagement of their kiss.

That should not be. She'd never heard tell of a mortal man immune to a swan maid's kiss.

Begobs! she thought, mimicking Gibbers. *Mayhap he is not mortal.*

Now, she ached to question him, but should she project her thoughts again? She had given him fair warning when he rode across the bridge. A warning he did not heed.

"Good night, milady." He bowed once, turned heel, and strode down the blind arcade.

Not ready to let him go, she conveyed her feelings to him. *Do not leave. I would willingly spend this night with you.*

He paused midstride and turned his head as if he'd not heard right, then he continued off.

Eithne jumped to her feet and ran to the doorway only to just glimpse his back disappearing down the stairwell. Who was he that he could ignore her heartfelt summons?

How dare he turn his back upon me. I have chosen him with my kiss! He cannot ignore me!

But he did. She glared at the chilling emptiness of the stonework. The sting of rejection did not sit well with her. It never had. Her life long she'd been rejected . . . she was ever the wicked "gurrul."

Standing in the doorway, she felt so deserted. Tears of futility clouded her eyes. She hated him for walking away . . . for turning his back upon her . . . but she hated herself more. She hated herself for seducing him . . . kissing him, entrapping him in the full moon sorcery of Rath Morna. Her hand gripped the door and she slammed it shut with such force that the resounding reverberation shook the candles in their sconces.

She stood abandoned in the middle of the most dismal of abodes. How she despised the cold stonework she stood upon. The gargoyles perched on each side of the hearth leered at her as if to say, "You are no different. You are evil and grotesque. This is where you belong."

Nay, she could not save this sea clansman from himself nor would she spend this night yearning for one who had outright rejected her. She was foolish to have kissed him, to allow herself to become entangled with him.

Her very silence condemned him to death. Yet, she had no choice. All the lives of those in Myr balanced against his own.

She walked slowly to the window cove.

An intense yearning for her mother's comforting arms and her consoling presence flooded Eithne. Stepping up on the stone seat, she thrust open the windows and breathed in the freshness of the night air. The stagnancy of Rath Morna suffocated and oppressed her.

The spring night called the wildness in her.

It was a night to fly. She would gather herself and transform. Flying above forest and fen, moor and meadow, again she would search for Ketha. Where had Sheelin imprisoned her? Where—?

The rush of wings drew Bron mac Llyr's attention. He lifted his gaze to see a great white swan fly across the face of the full moon. An omen of good luck he hoped. He would need good luck to find the swan healer, Ketha. He looked down at the illusion of his hand. It was amazing what appearances could do for a man . . . even false appearances. But he still could not play his harp nor wield a sword with the air of illusion.

Aye, that was his difficulty. It would be easy enough

for him to leap upon the enchanted Samisen and soar above the battlements of Rath Morna, but he could not do that until two mysteries were solved. The first was to find the whereabouts of Ketha. The second was to solve the riddle of Sheelin. Why did he so desire the speaking of the woman Eithne . . . if she were a woman at all?

It had taken some doing to leave her. Even now, his gaze traversed the keep towers to discern which was her window. Intrigue had nearly kept him at her side. In her regard, he'd chosen not to break the illusion, even though he easily countermanded the spell of her kiss by his own clarity. The instant her lips had touched his own, he knew the coming kiss was one of bewitchment. And in that moment he had allowed himself the dubious luxury of enchantment, but as a sea clansman and a son of Manannan mac Llyr, he was well versed in deflecting the spell craft of the sisterhoods.

His first love had been the sea nymph Sarenn. Her song had captured his innocent and youthful heart, luring him to her underwater abode where he remained a willing prisoner until his raging father appeared and freed him.

Bron knew enough of *fairy* women to keep his distance. He knew enough of mortal women to keep him inconstant. The worst and most telling battles of his life had been on the terrain of the heart. He'd spurned love and had been spurned in return . . . still he searched . . . for what he was not sure. There was an empty place within him that needed filling . . . that needed to love and be loved.

Mayhap the sea nymph Sarenn had spoiled him. Yet, what man in his right mind would risk involving himself with shape-shifting temptresses who could seduce him into unconsciousness.

Unfortunately, the mortal women he'd known had never compared to those of the otherworlds. Even so, the by-the-by occupation of a harper was dalliance and more than once his presence had caused a public swoon. He flirted with highborn ladies and lowly peasant maids. He'd an infallible instinct for intrigue and seduction.

And that was the rub. . . . Without a hand he could not play his harp . . . seduce or be seduced, nor could he enjoin in battle. His main life pursuits were at an end.

The thought depressed him mightily. He envisioned himself entering a holy order of hermits, or knitting with grandmothers, except that knitting required two hands. It seemed his arrival at Rath Morna was a presage. Here was his opportunity to save face . . . or better put, loose face by beheading.

Samisen whickered and shuffled to and fro impatiently in his stall. He looked over. Aye, he'd fallen into a dark hole of self-pity . . . the dark hole of Rath Morna.

He grimaced, seeing the stable for what it was, filthy and vermin infested. From the loft above, he could hear the loud snoring of Coup. He untied Samisen's halter and led him into the open air of the outer cashel. The stallion shook his mane with apparent relief.

"Take heart, our stay here will be naught more than

seven nights." He slipped a nose bag of grain over the horse's ears, spread out a woolen blanket, and lay down.

His arms behind his head, contemplating the starry night sky, he lightened his mood with thoughts of Lady Eithne. His mind lingered on the wild beauty whose eyes changed colors like marsh fire. She speaks with her eyes, he mused. She has no need of a voice.

Sheelin was quite the sorcerer to bring to form a woman who hauntingly matched Bron's ideal. The sunset halo of hair, skin so translucent she seemed fey which, he smiled to himself, was probably the case. He played with the vision of her true form. Mayhap she was an elemental . . . a tree or water sprite . . . or worse.

For now he would forestall unveiling the illusion. Life held enough disillusionment without fully tipping the cart. Yet, he must keep his clarity or the enchantment could consume him. Some men preferred to live out their lives in deception, he was not one. He chose to walk the earth awake and clear-eyed, taking full responsibility for his choices.

A part of him wished he might someday find a woman he might take into his heart. The woman Eithne in appearance beguiled him, charmed him, and seduced him, but he wanted more from a woman than bewitchment. He wanted honesty, full-bodied intimacy, and love without manipulation. He'd had enough of female manipulation through his escapades. He had also played the manipulator.

His own seventh sense told him that Eithne would be a mistress of manipulation. That knowledge intrigued him for life would never be dull in her midst. He had discovered that though she would not speak, the woman could throw her thoughts like a puppeteer. He wondered if it might work both ways. It could be diverting to dose her with her own brew. His gaze followed the glittering trails of shooting stars until he drifted into sleep.

Just before dawn, a putrid smell roused him to wakefulness. Opening his eyes, bulging luminous orbs peered into his own. "Arrah!" he growled, pushing a ghoulish face away.

"Begorrah, presarve me!" squealed the little beastie.

Bron sat up. "You queer devil. Who are you and what do you want?"

"I'm Gibbers and I'm seein' ye." He crouched in a lump like an obnoxious carbuncle.

"Why are you seeing me?" He examined him, realizing the bog creature was more pathetic than harmless.

"To see if yer nilly noggin will suit me."

"Are we to switch heads?"

"Musha, don't insult me!" he sniveled. "I meant for my bridge."

"Ahh!" said Bron, with slow dawning in his voice. "You must be the bridge troll."

"I am. And ye are Bron mac Llyr, another fool doomed to die fer the wicked gurrul Eithne."

"Eithne, wicked? Why say you that?"

"Och, look at my bridge. 'Tis all her refusin' to do her father's will. Ssshe's a wicked, wicked gurrul. Full of mischiefs and magics . . . Be warned, Bron mac Llyr."

"And what is her father's will?"

"Sssure yer knowin' it. The druid wishes her to speak. Och, 'tis a mistake. The tongues that wimmin have! Begobs, they're sharper than a dragon's tooth."

"Why does he wish it so?"

"Ask yer questions to the wicked gurrul. I'll not tell more. I want yer nilly noggin fer my bridge."

"At least you are truthful. But I have no plans to adorn your bridge."

"Ye shid be honored."

"Hah! If it is such an honor, then put your own head on a pike."

Gibbers frowned darkly. "Yer a rudie to say it. It cud not sarve me."

Bron laughed. "Nor would it serve me either. On that basis we should be friends. Surely you have more pastimes than waiting for poor fools to lose their heads?"

"Indade, I do." He grinned, exposing nothing but toothless gum. "I be a collector of sssecrets."

"Whose? Your own?"

"Nay! I've naught one tell-tale of me own."

"That surprises me."

"It shidn't."

"Are you a teller of secrets as well?"

He laughed with a kind of glee, and gurgle bubbled from his mouth. "Niver! They'd not be sssecrets then."

"I suppose not," admitted Bron, feeling as if someone had just touched his shoulder. He turned his head. He saw no one. Puzzled, his gaze left Gibbers and his eyes were drawn to the keep. He saw her. The Lady Eithne stood in full view from her high window.

"The wicked gurrul wantsss ye," hissed Gibbers, his voice oozing with salacious innuendo.

Bron turned back to Gibbers. "And she shall have me, but on my own terms. Can you keep that secret, Gibbers?"

"I cun. But again be warned, Bron mac Llyr, her heart is a cold pitatie."

"I care not. It's not her heart I am after."

"Thin what are ye afther?"

"My hand . . . a harper is no harper without a hand. I must find the healer Ketha."

Gibber's eyes livened. "Ketha?" he echoed.

"Aye, Ketha," returned Bron suspecting that like everyone else at Rath Morna, Gibbers knew something about Ketha. "I was told by a seeress that she alone in Banba could restore my hand."

"Yer hand looks fine to me."

Bron spread his fingers and chuckled. "'Tis Sheelin's illusion. I am not the whole fool. And I know you know more than you let on. Tell me, what do you know of Ketha?"

"Naught that I will tell."

He wanted to reach out and squeeze his scrawny little throat into speech. Irritation marked Bron's words. "You are a confessed knower of secrets. Ketha is one of those secrets I'll wager."

"Wager all ye wan. I cun be as mute as yer wicked gurrul."

Bron gave him a slow, tolerant smile.

Gibbers smiled back . . . more a grimace than a smile. The troll was shrewd, but he was bound to have at least one weakness which might loosen his blaggard's tongue and Bron vowed to discover it.

He rubbed his stomach. "I am hungry. Is there something truly edible within these cashel walls? I want no more of Sheelin's gross cookery."

"Ask the gurrul to sarve ye. 'Tis anythin' ye wish fer seven days and nights. Plaze yerself. See." He pointed a bollyworm finger. "Ssshesss wantin' ye still."

Bron looked back over his shoulder. Her silhouette filled the arch of the open window. He turned full around to face her and gave an exaggerated but graceful bow. "The sun rises on a new day, Lady Eithne," he shouted. "Let us meet in the feast hall."

Immediately, she disappeared from view. He thought like most women she would take time to prepare herself. He turned back to Gibbers . . . but he too had disappeared. Bron scanned the cashel yard. Where had the little beastie gone? He sniffed the air, allowing his nose to follow the sour scent of troll. A few steps away he discovered the long drag of his tracks, leading to the base of the stone wall. Surely he could not vanish into stone.

Samisen whinnied and nosed a clump of grass. Then Bron figured it out. He lifted the circular clod of grass and discovered a sinkhole through which a mush boned troll could slither and be gone.

Eithne raced through the all but deserted hall. Her teeth clenched together in anger, she dashed outside and down the steps of the keep. She wanted none of Gibbers's interference. What had he told Bron mac Llyr?

Filled with indignation she stomped past the warrior.

"Good morn, milady." His voice was hospitable but she did not even deign to give him a look. She fell onto her knees and peered down into the dank earth of the sinkhole.

Hear me, Gibbers! I'll not have it! Ye've snooped and stirred in my affairs enough! Come within the cashel walls again and I'll set Sheelin's hounds upon ye!

"He is gone," supplied Mac Llyr behind her.

Not for long, the little wart, she fumed inwardly, knowing he would be back to stir the pot of intrigue. He fed on gossip like other people did on food.

Mac Llyr was at her side, offering her a hand up. She ignored it and came to her feet under her own power.

"Did you rest well?" he asked kindly.

She cast him a dismissing glance—the one Sheelin often used upon her which made her feel no bigger than the fleas upon the hide of the Fir Darrig. She'd spent many an hour perfecting it in front of her looking glass and now at last she'd an occasion to use it.

While she flew last night, she'd sorted it all out. She'd made a decision to behave rudely to Bron mac Llyr . . . more rudely than she'd behaved to any of the others. This way he could not charm her, woo her, and win her sympathy. Why ever would he want to? Except to save his own life. He cared not a whit for her . . . no one at Rath Morna did. His gallantries were only motivated by his desire to survive.

When Coup severed his head, she would not shed a tear or feel a single pang of emotion. She would hold her features as frozen as the gargoyles on the cashel battlements. Aye, she'd worked it through and had her plan.

She stole a glance over her shoulder to see if he dared to follow her and force upon her his attentions. What she glimpsed was him standing before his horse, scratching its nose.

Humph! she thought. *He lets me walk away. He is the biggest fool of all!*

Chapter
4

Bron watched the shimmer of the setting sun on the western horizon, his eyes watering from the brilliance. It shone with the dazzling radiance of polished gold. Beside him on the high cashel wall sat Coup de Grace; like Bron, his legs dangled over the edge.

"'Tis like seeing there and beyond," said Coup philosophically, nursing a gourd of brew. "I've never missed a sunset in all my time at Rath Morna."

"And how long has that been?" asked Bron, reaching out of habit with his sword hand for the gourd. His fingers passed right through it. Muttering under his breath, he switched hands and successfully brought the gourd to his mouth and took a long pull. The fire of it near burned through his gullet, but tonight he felt the need to numb his senses and to put to rest the harpies of his mind. He was homesick for the sea . . . for the bite of a rousing gale, the crash of waves on ragged cliffs, and the cree of a hundred gulls soaring in a snapping blue sky.

"I know naught. I've always been here." Coup scratched his bearded face.

Bron stared over at him curiously. Did all those enslaved in Sheelin's court believe so? He handed the gourd to Coup and asked, "Then you know something of Lady Eithne."

"I know she is a witch and loves nothing more than tricking lads like yerself to a misfortunate end." His voice dropped to a whisper. Furtively, he leaned closer to Bron, shielding his mouth with his hand. "There's no cure for wickedness. Keep yer wits about ye or she'll trip you into a pretty puddle."

"What are you saying?"

"I'm a saying when you go to her at night be prepared for her sorcery. All know she's a shape-shifter."

"Have you seen her shape shift?"

"Nay, but all tell they've never seen the like of beasties she can become. And the secret ye must know is how to handle yerself."

"Oh? What must I do?" asked Bron. He was surprised that the Lady Eithne had such a reputation among the weird monstrosities of the court. It was like the crow calling the raven black.

"Ye must hold her tight no matter what happens, for that is the only way to save yerself."

Bron was becoming quite mellow from the ale. He chuckled. "'Twill not be so unpleasant a task to hold her close."

Coup sneered. "Aye, especially when she rips out yer gizzard."

"And would she do that?"

"Aye! And more. Take heed. 'Tis not every man gets the advantage of my counsel. Drink nothing she gives

41

you. Never shut yer eyes in her presence or ye might open them to find yerself changed into a wee toad."

The image brought a smile to Bron's lips. He reached again for more drink. "It might not be such a bad life to be a wee toad in the pocket of Lady Eithne."

"Hah!" spat Coup. "She'd toss you into a cauldron of witch's brew or dry ye in the sun till ye crackled. Mark me, she's a heart stealer. 'Tis her kiss, they say. She kisses ye and yer naught but buzzard bait. You'll pass yer seven days in heaven and then it will be too late to do naught but have me chop off yer head. Like the others, you'll think she loves ye true and will speak in the last instant. But she will not. She'll hold her lips tight as a virgin's thighs."

"Arrah . . . that tight?" Bron was fast on his way to being tipsy.

"That tight!" confirmed Coup.

"Well, it appears I must work upon a plan to woo this lady without losing my own heart to her witchery."

"I've not much hope for ye."

"Hope is naught but nostalgia for the future," enlightened Bron, rising to his feet. He teetered dangerously on the edge of the high stone wall, underestimating the potency of the brew he'd been drinking.

Coup grabbed his calf in an attempt to steady him. "Ye'll have us both tumbling o'er the edge."

Bron squatted back on his heels and surveyed the distance to the keep and announced to Coup, "I calculate I might enter the Lady Eithne's window with a little genius, a little daring, and a length of rope." Of course he was not sure how much of his genius could be attributed to the false courage of Coup's sour brew.

"And why would ye want to do that? What's wrong with using the stairs and stepping through her doorway?" questioned Coup, shifting his own position away from the edge.

"The element of surprise!"

"Aye, ye'll be surprised when she pushes ye back out her window and ye've but one hand to hang on with." Coup laughed hard at his own jest.

Bron grinned himself, but somewhere deep inside he felt a sharp pang of defeat. He glanced down at the illusion of his hand. What Coup said was true . . . a one-handed man did not scale tower keeps and climb into fair maidens' windows. The thought sobered him and he jumped to safe footage on the battlement walk. Slowly, he out-breathed a deep felt despair and ponderously watched the last purple lights of twilight succumb to darkness.

Mayhap he should leave Rath Morna tonight and return home to the sea. He'd not be a whole man, but he'd be a man like any other who had gone to battle and been maimed. He'd no need to entangle himself with sorcerers and witches in the hope of finding someone who could heal him. He knew the truth of it . . . that it was only a false hope that kept him searching, and the shame of standing before his father's clan without a sword hand.

His attention was caught by the movement in a window opening high in the keep tower. The window casement framed Lady Eithne's silhouette. What was the mystery in her that drew him . . . called him? Did it really matter that she might be an illusion? Might all life be illusion? He did not know. But in this inescapable moment the flame-haired witch summoned him as surely as a full-faced moon rose on the horizon. He felt her call in his mind, his loins, and most fully in his heart.

Eithne was beginning to hate the power a luminous moon held over her. She felt distracted and restlessly wild. She ran her fingers through her hair and reached her arms high in a full sensuous stretching while her bare feet danced over the floor in disconnected patterns. A part of her wanted to hide under the bedding of her pallet until morning, but the other part shamelessly lusted for the sea clansman.

A knock vibrated the thickness of her door. Her feet halted. Had she heard right? Again the knock sounded. She clutched her belly with nervousness. It won't be him, she told herself . . . and if it is I will refuse to open the door. Yet, her feet betrayed her and she found her fingers reaching for the great ring latch.

The door yawned open.

He stood there. She experienced a flash of fear like no other in her life. His gaze rested lightly upon her. She dared not meet his eyes. Instead she picked out the details of his tunic, his boots, his belt, and lastly the tousled queue of black hair partly looped over his broad shoulder. She couldn't even think of what to do next.

"Milady, might I enter your chamber this night?" he asked without pretension.

As if drugged, she assented with a slow nod of her head, though she knew she had no choice but to allow it. It took a very long time for her to move back and give him space to pass through. It took even a longer time for him to come forward.

When at last he did, her heart did a small cartwheel and she wished she was anywhere but there. But for his missing hand his body was perfection. As he moved . . . aye, he knew how to move . . . with each gesture . . . each step a masculine vibrancy emanated from him. There was no standing with his jaw askew like the others. This one was accustomed to entering ladies' chambers and that reality fired her fear even more.

He walked over to the open window. Standing with his back to her, he gazed out. "A lovely night," he remarked, turning to face her. He looked her straight in the eyes.

How she fought to keep her equanimity. Never, never had she felt so exposed. What did he see when he watched her? Did he see she was the "wicked gurrul"? Had Gibbers told him of her evil deeds? How she had allowed all those men to die, never shedding a single tear.

From shame she averted her eyes to a flickering candle in the wall sconce just behind him. Oddly, like a puff of breath, a breeze rushed through the open window and snuffed out the candle. With no fire in the hearth, the room fell into darkness but for the moonlight streaming across the floor.

Between them the air hung thick with mystery, expectation, and hazard. He moved. The light traced his profile that held the arrogance of lineage and the confidence of experience. Coming to her with a noiseless stride, he caught her in his arms.

His sudden proximity was a shock. She pushed against his chest with the palms of her hands, but he did not relinquish his hold.

Softly he said, "Is this not what you wanted, milady?"

Her throat dry as ash, she shook her head in a weak protest, all the while realizing her error in snuffing the candle. This action had misled him. He brought his hand to tilt her face, his broad palm at the base of her throat. His arm tightened her to his body.

Not a kiss, she thought. Another kiss would disassemble her . . . she'd be a quivering pudding at his feet.

It was pure fear that spurred her into the use of magic. Between one breath and the next she transformed, not into a swan but a snarling lioness with barbed tail and triple rows of fangs. Instantly, she felt him release his hold upon her.

In a deep-voiced blur he uttered words she could not understand. Just as suddenly, a gust of whirlwind filled the room and the window clamored shut. Shockingly, the sea clansman himself transformed into a savage, thick-pelted, lean-flanked, broad-shouldered black wolf. The beast snapped and growled.

Taken aback and unable to hold her illusion for more than mere seconds, Eithne changed again into a giant serpent that coiled threateningly, shooting out its forked tongue.

The air sparked. Hackles raised, the wolf yawned a

full-throated howl and attacked, its white fangs gripped her coiling tail.

Blessed goddess! Eithne wondered what she'd gotten herself into. She quickly changed back into her own form and scrambled up a decorative hearth pilaster to the nearest sanctuary, the wide mantel ledge. Precariously she held fast to the head of an ornamental sylph and peered down at the black wolf.

Red jaws agape, a menacing growl rumbled from his barrel chest. Too late Eithne realized that on the whole her shape-shifting had been an exercise in bad judgment.

Was she to spend the remainder of her life upon the hearth mantel? Tentatively, she lowered her foot. She saw the snap of jaws and felt the steam of hot breath upon her toes. Hastily, she yanked back her foot.

Bron mac Llyr did not play fair. She had a mouthful of epithets to say to that, but as always she would not. Instead, she would most likely pop out with hives. That always seemed to happen when she had something important to say and never said it. Aye, she must wait the spriggan out.

She shifted.

She shifted again.

She changed position once more. Her left leg was going numb.

Her lips tightened with aggravation. She glared at the wolf with her most withering gaze . . . the one that caused those that walked, to crawl, and those that crawled, to slither.

The black wolf's response was an indifferent yawn. In her desperation she considered transforming into her swan self and flying out the window. Unfortunately, the window was across the room and now shut. Even so, she didn't think it was a good idea to give her complete set of tricks away all at once.

Time passed. The black wolf had relaxed on his haunches, fiery eyes alert. What was he waiting for? A bone?

And then it occurred to her that he held her hostage in a clever scheme to make her speak.

Begorrah and begobs! She would not!

What she wanted to give him was a piece of her mind . . . but from spite she would not . . . at least not yet.

There are times, even though trapped and cornered, self-will is stronger. She adjusted this way and that until her length was supported by the mantel and her shoulders by the sylph. The wolf's black-lined eyes followed her movements shrewdly. If need be, she would remain a statuesque fixture on the hearth until she turned to stone. Closing her eyes with exaggerated sufferance, she endured. . . .

. . . but only until she dozed off.

Eithne landed hard, so hard that when she hit the cold slate floor, her teeth nearly snapped off her tongue and the black wolf near snapped off her head.

She might have screamed if her breath hadn't been knocked out of her. She might have leaped up if the wolf hadn't been straddling her, its fangs teasing her throat. Instead, she lay still staring into green-fire orbs.

Then it wasn't the wolf's fangs on her neck but the teeth and hot breath of Bron mac Llyr. His dark head raised up, his features appeared wolfen. A primitive fire glittered in his brooding, hooded eyes. She struggled against him, not realizing her efforts only inflamed him all the more. His weight, he balanced upon his elbows, but she felt the full-bodied pressure of his hips on her own.

It was shocking enough to discover a fleering wolf on top of her, but in comparison the wolf was less threatening than Bron mac Llyr. Fisting her hands, she thrust her strength against his chest. He did not budge. What was he trying to prove? That he was stronger?

His hand was in her hair, grasping the side of her face, brushing back the long copper strands, his mouth brutally capturing her own. She twisted her face away. His mouth at her throat, he kissed and tongued the curve of her neck. She writhed and struggled, but the muscular hardness of his arms contained her. He was so powerful, she felt the heaving of his chest pressing her own, and her breath coursed as if she'd been running fast.

With low laughter he caught both her wrists in the grip of his one hand and brought her knuckles to his lips, nipping them roughly.

The realization hit Eithne that he'd not quite fully transformed from wolf. Great goddess! Hadn't he revenge enough? Now, she must be chased about her chambers by a wolfman.

Uttering a growl, he lowered his head and clamped his teeth into the loose fabric of her bodice. He tore the garment open and exposed her breasts to his burning gaze. His nostrils flared . . . and so did

Eithne's temper. Her bosom heaved with indignation. She glared at him steadily as her cheeks suffused with a raw blush.

His eyes narrowed wickedly.

Her resistance did not falter while she quickly concluded she must use her own wiles to keep him at bay. Valiantly, she used the last vestige of her energy to transform one last time.

She reared up with all her might. The air crackled and she felt power surge through her limbs as she reshaped into a talon-clawed, carnelian-scaled winged dragon.

In pooling moonlight, Bron mac Llyr lay sprawled on the floor, openmouthed, staring up at her. Saffron flame glimmered from her fanged jaws. Through red reptilian eyes she leered down at him, witnessing him shift full shape again to wolf. His shoulders rippled beneath the shiny black pelt, his jaw lengthened and narrowed in a jagged-toothed gape, and his emerald eyes smoldered canine venery.

She knew she had only seconds to execute her plan. In that instant she returned to her own shape and she moved for the water pitcher. The black wolf lunged toward her. She let fly the water. It hit him full face.

'Twas the man that crashed into her, knocking her sideways and to the floor. She lay stunned.

Drenched, he stepped toward her. He wiped his face with his sleeve and pulled back his long hair from wild disarray.

"Arra-a-ah! Forgive me, milady," he apologized profusely, bending down on one knee to her. "The game was more dangerously played than I supposed."

Water dripped off his chin and beaded off the end of his nose.

Eithne sat up and clutched together her ripped bodice. She experienced some guilt in that she had started it all, but she would hardly confess it.

In the end he did the civilized thing. He lit a candle and looked about for a covering for her. He retrieved a blanket from her pallet that he wrapped around her shoulders. She accepted his attentions, choosing to make the most of her advantage.

"Oh," he said with concern. "You're bleeding, milady."

She looked down and saw the red smear on her shoulder. His fingers were carefully parting the hair on the back of her head. Wholly drained, she sat with her lips in a disgruntled pout and endured. This seemed to be the night for it.

"Aye, 'tis a brave goose egg and a wee wound. Fortunately, none of my doing."

She cast him an accusing glance. Of course it was his doing. He'd kept her perched on the hearth for what seemed like hours.

Her recriminatory look caused him to amend his words. "Aye, 'twas somewhat my fault."

While she changed her shift, he courteously turned away. They moved to sit on the pallet. He proved himself an apt caretaker by holding a damp compress of cold water upon her injury while he recounted a few of his own . . . including the one that caught Eithne's main interest—the event of his losing his sword hand.

She lay on her stomach beside him, her cheek pillowed on her arm. He carefully parted her hair away from the swelling lump and said, "Aye, it was close to evening on the fifth day of battle. The slaughter had been terrible. Pride and shame were there side by side and hardness and red anger, and there was blood on the white skin of young fighting men. And the dashing of spear against shield, and sword against sword, and shouting of the fighters and the whistling of arrows and the rattling of scabbards was like thunder over the plains. Many a time I slipped in the blood that was under my feet, and believed I'd not be able to lift my sword arm one more time, so exhausted was I."

He paused and she sensed in his mind the endarkened visions sweeping past. "Countless fell and the river carried away the bodies of friends and enemies together." Regret seared his voice.

"The Fomorians are a fierce and frightening lot of creatures. Some have but a single leg and a single eye. Some have men's bodies, but walk upright on flipperlike feet." She felt the pressure of his hand lift from her head and then his fingers began stroking her upper back. He was probably not even aware of doing it and she hoped he would not stop.

"It was twilight on the seventh day. The battle had been won by my people, the Tuatha de Danann, and the Fomorians were in retreat. 'Tis my task as a harper to walk the battlefield playing the *coronach* or spirit-call to the souls of my dead clansmen. In this way all find safe return to the faraway isles where they spend their next existence in peace and abundance."

His hands felt warm on Eithne's shoulders. The

contact had seemed almost reluctant affection and gave her a sensation of light-headedness that she made a concentrated effort not to show.

"Of the thousands of bodies strewn over the landscape most were dead, but I heard moaning. My search took me to the edge of the battlefield. There I knelt down to hold the head of one dying youth. His golden hair was clotted with his own blood. He was of the sea clans. I spoke a hoarse 'fare-thee-well and be proud' and invoked him to let loose his spirit and return home. He died. I turned his body to the direction of the western sea and I slipped my cloak off my shoulders and covered him."

The sorrow in Bron's voice brought a swelling to Eithne's own throat. She wondered why men fought such battles and over what? But she did not ask.

He continued, "I picked up my harp again. Nearby I could see shadows and hear movement in the fallen leaves. I peered through the closely woven branches, but could only make out vague shapes. That instant, I was hit from behind and when I regained my wits, I was on my knees surrounded by gibbering, squealing, Fomorian warriors. Looking up, I faced their chieftain in his battle chariot.

"He glared at me from an enormous eye. 'Who are you?' he asked in a garbled voice. I dared not tell him for if he knew my lineage I would be killed at once. I kept my mouth shut. 'Twas my misfortune to crosspath with them as they fled. Even as we spoke, they surveyed the battlefield from fear of pursuit. 'Twas plain the chieftain sought one last revenge and 'twould be my head . . . until he saw the harp. The Fomorian are a bloodless race and have no continuity or life after death.

"With a single command from him, my arm was held out. Yelling out an exultant cry, his sword came down and sliced off my hand."

Bron's voice halted.

Eithne winced inwardly at the cruelty of the Fomorian's deed. She turned over, gently touched Bron's sword hand, and looked up at him. His unfocused eyes glistened with moisture. She did not know what to do . . . but instinctively she reached for him.

When Eithne's arms encircled Bron, he became suddenly aware that he had held his shock and his grief inside all this time. He had needed to tell this story to someone. Contact with her body relaxed him and brought about a surrender within him that was long overdue. Feelings had been tapped inside him that he had spent months trying to suppress. The hideous visions of what he'd experienced in battle were revealed and released. He buried his face into the cloud of her hair and allowed the tears of deeper emotion to flow. Whoever or whatever she was, she was there. The slow rise and fall of her breathing, the beating of her heart all washed over and enfolded him like a golden net from the sea.

Chapter

5

Eithne woke to whistling, directly in her left ear. The sound was lilting and lighthearted. She cracked open her eyes. The room danced with morning sun. All came back to her as she found herself curled on her side and pillowed on the arm of Bron mac Llyr. Embarrassingly, one of her legs was looped between his own.

"A new day to you, milady," he said with a lopsided smile that was just sardonic enough to disarm her.

Her first inclination was to jump up, but the chamber was chilly and beneath the blanket his body radiated warmth. Even so, she withdrew her leg. Now, the only trace of the black wolf was the mussed up tangle of his long dark hair. It was queer to be sleeping beside the same man who had almost shredded her to bits a few hours before and then confessed his innermost wounds.

"How is your head?" he asked in a tone of genuine concern.

She reached up, gingerly touched the lump on the back of her head, and grimaced.

"Aye, 'twill be sore." His arm shifted and his fingers patted her hair gently. She felt his sincerity, a rare commodity at Rath Morna.

"We best be awake and at it, milady." He carefully slipped his arm from beneath her head and sat up. She watched as he shook his hair off his shoulders and winged his muscled arms to wakefulness. "Have you a hairbrush?"

She nodded and moved her gaze to the small dressing table in one corner of the room. If he had one vanity, she realized it must be his hair.

He crossed the room.

He picked up the hairbrush, but paused, and studied curiously the various vials and bottles on the dressing table. He took the glass stopper from a vile of scent and sniffed. His dark brows lifted with approval and he dabbed some on the hollow of his throat.

Eithne could not help but smile. The sweet fragrance was one that markedly attracted bees, butterflies, and woodland fairy folk. She dared not wear it out-of-doors.

Finally, he sat on the single stool and unwound his braid slowly, pulling the brush through his hair with irritated strokes.

Eithne took pity on him and came to her feet. She crossed over to him and put a halting hand upon his own. He looked up at her, reading the unspoken offer in her eyes and gave up the hairbrush readily.

"Aye, 'tis a woman's touch it needs. I would long ago have cut it, but the men of my clan wear their hair thus."

The braid had set waves in his hair and as she

combed it out it clicked and sparked. Something inside her clicked and sparked as well. His nearness became as beckoning as a half-heard call. A connective current danced over the hairbrush and across her fingers. With supreme difficulty she managed to keep on the task, loving the feel of his silky hair. Her own hair was unruly with curl and more nearing the texture of a pony's mane.

Patiently, she smoothed out the tangles. She gave him more attention than she needed to. Almost playfully, she ran her hand under his hair and wound its raven flow around her wrist, then opened her hand and let it fall in cascading waves to dust the floor.

Carefully, she divided his hair into three thick strands and began to plait. Then her hands bound the ends with a leather thong. A sign she'd completed her task, she snapped the length of his thick braid like a whip against his back.

"Arrah." He laughed. "You'll not strangle me with my own hair I hope." He looked up at her flirtatiously and let flash his white teeth in a warming smile.

He might be immune to her kiss, but she was not immune to his charm. She turned away and raised the hairbrush to her own hair. She felt a halting hand upon her own.

"Milady, can I repay the favor?"

His fingers cupped her hand a long moment. With a half-headed nod she relinquished the hairbrush to his hold. He stood and moved behind her. The instant he touched the strands of her hair something shocked through her. Gently, he brushed, taking more care than a doting nanny.

"'Tis a fiery mass you wear upon your head. I fear just touching you will set me aflame." He had pulled back her hair on one side and leaned to speak these words in her ear. The heat of his breath caused her skin to tingle and fluttery sensations to whirl in her stomach. She was the one aflame and had been since first she set eyes on him. He drew away and let loose her hair. It fell and splayed over her shoulders and down past her waist. She was not ready for him to be finished.

He had gone to the window and opened it. He leaned out saying, "There is nothing like a spring morning to fill a man with life and wonder." Then he turned around. "If you are the one to provide for my needs . . . my need at this moment is food. But only under stipulation that I will see it prepared from scratch even if I must crack the eggs and knead the bread myself. Please lead me to the kitchens, milady."

She studied him, her eyes narrowed cannily. Why would he say this unless he could see through Sheelin's illusions? Light raining down upon him, he returned her probing gaze with an affable smile. He was indeed handsome, but there was more to him than bold good looks. The darkness that permeated everything at Rath Morna somehow did not touch him. Something about him, she could not quite put her finger on it, was immune.

Aye, it was a new day and a new adventure. She would take him to the kitchens. She bid him to follow with a curt wave of her hand.

He followed, a lilting tune upon his lips as she pulled open the great oak door and led him down the spiraling stairs, through the deserted feast hall and out into the yard. Softly whistling, he followed beneath the connecting stone arches of the inner bailey toward the brewery house.

The kitchen and storage buildings were situated beside the brewery house and linked to the banquet hall by an underground tunnel. She pushed on the door and cracked it only enough to spy the hairy flank of a fat sow blocking the entrance. Twice she pushed on the door, but could not budge it or the sow.

"Allow me, milady," offered Mac Llyr. He stepped forward and thrust full force a broad shoulder against the door. Eithne heard the disgruntled snort of the sow as the door yawned open. Dislocated piglets scurried between her feet. Bron muttered something about his breakfast escaping right before his eyes.

Despite herself, Eithne smiled. He returned the smile and bowed gallantly, while she stepped through the doorway. "We have breached the wicket and rousted the bacon."

The kitchens were deserted and less than tidy. In truth, it appeared more the barnyard than the kitchen. Chickens roosted in cupboards, mouse tracks dusted the work surfaces, and ants trooped across the chopping block. Eithne poked through wilted greens and fruit rotting in baskets, her nostrils pinched with disgust. In the end, it came to sifting weevils from flour and stealing eggs from a hen's nest in the hearth pot.

"I would help, if you but show me what to do," he offered. Obliging, Eithne plopped the dough in front of him and pointed. "And what am I to do with it?"

Of course he knew what he was to do with it! Eithne wriggled her fingers motioning that he should knead it.

"Ah," he said, mimicking a dull wit. "You wish me to knead it. Why didn't you just say so?"

Not amused, she turned away from him and began cracking eggs. But such a ruckus of pounding and thumping caused her to turn back.

The air clouded with flour dust as he vigorously kneaded the dough. He looked a graybeard. Eithne pinched her lips together squelching her mirth.

His eyes sparkled with tease. He picked up a handful of flour and puffed it right into her face.

She sneezed.

He laughed. "Among the sea clans sneezing is a favorable omen. It means your just due will come to you."

Aye, she thought, *and your just due will come to you, sea clansman.* Caught in the playfulness of the moment, she threw an egg at him. It splatted right in the middle of his forehead, trickling down his face.

Now it was she whose lips stretched wide in smile. He clowned for her, rubbing the dough and egg about his face. He growled and sputtered like the Fir Darrig in her father's Unseelie Court.

It felt good to smile. She could not remember when last she had truly smiled. He began throwing dough globs at her, which she caught and threw at him. He darted back and forth toward her with the mock ferociousness of a snarling wolf until she felt laughter rising in her belly.

"Have you had enough?" he asked jauntily.

She shook her head, her lips parted— And then, just as swiftly she clamped her hand over her mouth. She'd nearly spoken! He had taken her off guard. Her eyes met his. In the long moment she saw his delight and glimpsed something more. . . .

It had been so long . . . so long since she'd gazed into eyes that looked back. Was that why he was different from all the others?

He had continuity! He had said it himself the night before when he spoke of the bloodless Fomorians. Like those creatures, no one at Rath Morna had a soul. All were illusions. All were her father's illusions . . . perversions of his own twistedness. It made her heart sick to think of it.

"Milady? You are as wide-eyed as an owl at midnight. Is something wrong?" He stepped closer.

Eithne blinked once, then twice. And slowly shook her head wonderingly.

He reached, and with a single finger gently dusted the flour off the tip of her nose. He then leaned near and kissed the shined nub. It was a call for her attention. But her attention was in unraveling this puzzle. Why hadn't she seen the difference in the feast hall when she kissed him? Why hadn't she realized before?

"Milady?" Bron inquired again.

She focused her eyes fully on him.

Taking her hand he said, "Come, a meal here is not likely. I think we would do well to wash ourselves beyond the cashel walls and fend off the land. Show me your escape route from this prison. Surely you have one better than that little troll's sinkhole."

Eithne nodded, her eyes still delving his own.

"Lead on!" he rousted, putting his hands about her waist and abruptly facing her forward.

A thousand quandaries danced on the periphery of Bron's mind. He was not a man to play games, but he had now stepped into the most intriguing game of his life. Before him walked the woman of his dreams and that was exactly what she was . . . a dream, an illusion. After last night he could not doubt it. A mortal woman could not display such tricks. Mayhap he'd a weakness for nymphs, enchantresses, and witches.

He followed the apparition of his ideal through the cashel yard, down into the maze of lower dungeons of Rath Morna. He crawled behind her through a drain tunnel leading to the outer walls. Wiping the mud off his knees, he came to his feet on the banks of the moat.

Eerie mists shrouded the true brightness of the day. The buzzards on the bridge cawed and wing-flapped to flight. She lifted her skirts, a bare dainty foot peeked out, and before it disappeared into the murk, Bron glimpsed a skin of webbing between her toes. He'd not noticed this before—a freakish flaw was ever the giveaway of a witch. He paused and ruminated upon this discovery. Last night had been but a glimpse of the many guises she might take.

Something large and slithery passed through the greenish sludge, and Bron wondered if she could be of the same spawn. His ardor slightly dampened, he swallowed his disgust. He waded in, crossed the moat, and climbed up after her into a mist-free landscape.

For the first time since his arrival at Rath Morna he

breathed deeply, fully, and cleanly. Here the air was fragrant with spring and dewy morning.

To his relief she let her skirts drop, covering lithe, long legs. She hastened the pace. His boots sloshing, he matched her stride, stealing sidelong glances. She seemed to have quite the mind of her own. That she could not speak proved in his favor . . . or did it? He had felt the impact of her emotions and he could read her temper in the color of her changeling eyes.

Aye, she could be dangerous, he mused inwardly. Aye, but not as dangerous as he.

A brisk breeze whipped her skirts and free flying hair. Gray wing clouds flew on the horizon alerting Bron to the fickleness of the spring weather. Ahead, great stones rose up and captured Bron's full attention. He slowed, letting his gaze study the tall dolmens that stood on the heath like a circle of giant's teeth. 'Twas a holy henge. Such places were worshiped as hallowed ground by his own people.

He continued to follow Eithne as she threaded through the henge. He stooped to pass beneath the capstone lintels which linked the tall dolmens of this ancient site. Just beyond, he heard the splash of ducks taking flight from water.

She cast a glance over her shoulder and gestured to a small pond. He came beside her. On the tranquil silver water-mirror a mother duck and her new hatchlings paddled about on a morning outing. Along the banks lapwings and swifts perched on swaying reeds, chattering encouragingly.

Eithne stepped behind the fern cover in a shady copse and began taking off her clothing. He lowered his eyes, aggravated at his own response to her beauty. Walking away, he took a seat on a boulder. He pulled off his own boots, one by one, and let the green swamp water drizzle out. Through the clarity of the water he could see fish darting across the pond's bottom. Catching fish barehanded was a skill he perfected during his sojourn with Sarenn beneath the sea . . . though he'd never tried it one-handed. That would be his challenge of the day.

He lifted his head and his gaze strayed to Eithne. She undressed as easily as if she were a sea snake shedding scales . . . mayhap she was. Yet, with womanly grace she stretched her arms skyward and gave a freeing sigh. Her red hair gleamed like polished copper and her fair skin glowed golden.

She stepped into the pond like a selkie into the sea. He knew beneath the illusion she must be water beast or fairy . . . no matter she was full of mischief and even treachery. Her head turned to him and her eyes flashed an undeniable invitation . . . an arrow of seduction, one aimed not to his heart, but well beneath.

Now, he thought. Now was the time to expose her. Now was the time he should break the veil of illusion. Yet, all he wanted to see was the perfect curve of her smooth hips, the flowing arch of her neck, and the dusty rose of her lips. Again, for reasons dark and light, he chose not to see past that. He looked instead down, seeing the illusion of wholeness of his sword hand which held form even beyond the sorcery of Rath Morna. And he knew the illusion held because he chose it to be so. And for now he would see Eithne as she was this moment . . . a beautiful woman, one he desired. Between one breath and the next, he surrendered to his own loneliness, his own need to love and his own woundedness that yearned for healing.

'Twas midday when Eithne walked up the mossy bank to where Bron roasted a thornback toadfish on a smoldering alderwood fire. The smell filled her nostrils, but she was not tempted in the least because she was not a meat eater. During her swim she'd satisfied her hunger by eating watercress and she'd munched on wild asparagus growing along the shore while watching Mac Llyr attempt to catch a fish single-handedly. When at last he did, she applauded happily. He'd persevered and succeeded. She admired this . . . she admired him.

Tiny blue-winged creatures fluttered in the curling smoke around Bron. He batted at them with annoyance. She squinted, trying to determine whether they be fairy folk or butterflies. 'Twas the scent he'd dabbed on himself which drew them. If they were fairy folk, he must share his bounty.

He looked up at her. His expression was pleasant and warming. So warming, that it dispersed the threat of a storm gathering in the dark clouded sky above them and the chill of the cold water beading upon her bare skin. She bent to pick up her chemise, slipped it over her head, and then laced herself into her starflower embroidered over gown.

"We have guests for dinner," he said. Her head snapped around quickly under his sea green gaze. He was canny about everything she realized . . . maybe even about her. His eyes left hers and followed the opalescent shimmer of the blue-winged fairy folk.

A feminine voice sounded out of nowhere, "Mayhap we should invite them to help themselves." Eithne looked around with puzzlement, first to the winged fairy folk, then over her shoulder to the surrounding woods.

Staring straight at her, Bron replied, "Do you think it? What if they make gobblers of themselves? They'll naught be enough for you and me."

Eithne glowered. Who was he talking to?

The mysterious voice came again, "I'll not want a fairy curse upon me because I could not share. I have enough troubles with my father's evil magics."

Her mouth dropped open. The devil! He could throw his voice!

She watched a triumphant mischief mark his strong features. With his knife tip he expertly procured a tasty morsel of fish from the fire and offered it to her. "Milady."

Her lips tightened, her emotions a slow boil. She did not like to be teased nor did she like someone else putting words into her mouth . . . even though she put none there herself.

"Arrah, milord. You partake first. I will feast upon your leavings." She heard his mimicking sweet mew.

That was beyond the beyond.

Enough! her mind shouted at him.

His features winced. She knew her message was received. Once she used her powers to project her thoughts, her meaning could not be misconstrued.

Fully opening to him she went on, *If you are to speak for me at least speak true . . . not toady words of a pudding-mouthed maid who has no spittle.*

"And have you spittle?" was his laconic answer as he put the refused morsel of fish to his own lips.

Beway, I do! And a tongue of fire that goes with it! You pandering excuse for a sea clansman.

"Then use it!" he said emphatically, his eyes now sharp with challenge. "That I might be gone and away from this misfortunate place. Or do you receive perverse pleasure in seeing heads roll at your unhuman feet?"

Eithne looked down at her feet. She straightened, her chin tilted just so with haughty affront. *My unhuman feet? At least I have two hands. Can you boast as much? I do not persecute your own deformity. Instead, the first night I invited you to my chambers . . . you are the one who refused. Am I not good enough for the likes of a one-handed man?*

By now they were within inches of each other. The closure of space between had just happened. Eithne was not aware of moving. She was only aware of his heat, his scent, and the deep throttle of his voice.

"Arrah! You are more than good enough. But I'm not a man to lose his head over a lass."

Then flee! You can. We are outside the cashel walls of Rath Morna. You are no longer a prisoner. Why do you stay?

"I stay because I do not go," he said cryptically.

Her eyes narrowed. *Then you are a victim of enchantment like the rest of us.*

"Nay, not I."

She curled her lip in a delicate sneer. *Then why do you stay?*

His white straight teeth flashed challengingly. "You are a snoop of a lass, like your little bog wart troll."

Eithne's features slipped to a pout. *Do not compare me to the likes of him.*

"Then you are not kith or kin?"

She shook her head emphatically. *Nay, we are not. Why would you think it? Do I look like him?*

"By no means. At least not in your present form. But in a place such as Rath Morna seeing is not believing."

You are a canny one . . . and the first to be so.

"Only as long as I keep my head," he said ruefully.

She did not smile. The thought of him losing so pleasing a face hurt her heart.

His gaze held her full attention, breath after breath. What arresting eyes he had. What faraway shores and sights had they beheld? It would be too, too wicked for those sea clan eyes to end up buzzard bait. And those sea clan lips . . . only a wisp of scar marred their perfect form. So close to him and so drawn, she could not help but reach out and lightly touch that place upon his mouth. It was a faint reminder that the world was never safe.

She wanted to confess to him her loneliness and her knowingness that he was different from the others . . . that she knew he was not a conjured vision of her father's black arts. But dare she? She could not give away her own secrets. What if he was in league with her father? Yes, he might have a soul, but so did her father . . . and this sea clansman seemed more than knowledgeable about magic. After last night she realized he was a sorcerer himself. He proved immune to her kiss. She could not trust a man who was immune to the very essence of her power. She made to step away.

"No." His voice was huskily halting. He caught her fingers within his own and drew them to the rough sand of his cheek. "Feel me. I'm no illusion of your father's court. I am a man of bone and flesh."

Frightened, she tried to retract her fingertips, but he held them fast. On all levels she wished he were an illusion. Illusions could be walked through and dissolved like vapor into the air. Illusions could be ignored, laughed at, or re-created in a less threatening form.

And what was threatening about Bron mac Llyr? All and everything! Unlike the others, when he touched her, her unaccustomed senses blazed. Unlike the others when she met his eye, she saw depth and soul. Unlike the others he was alive and passionately so. Vibrancy marked his every stride and leaped from the sculpted features of his emboldened face.

"You wanted me well enough the past two nights."

'Tis only your conceit that tells you so, she sent clearly in the flat emotion of a slug, just squashed. She knew that now the full moon was past so would be her yearnings . . . or were they?

He relinquished her hand and brought his own to tilt her face, his broad palm cushioning her chin. "Nevertheless, 'tis my turn to kiss you."

She did not like this maneuver much, because

something was happening to her that was beyond her control . . . and Eithne did not like being out of control. It had been her only defense against the magics of Rath Morna and now it should be her defense against the charms of Bron mac Llyr.

She forced herself to meet his gaze and she would, with a mere thought, catapult her rejection like a quiver of icicles aimed straight to his heart. But before she gathered herself, his lips came down upon her own.

His were moist and warm, hers were dry and cold. *I will not feel,* she vowed inwardly . . . but feel she did . . . soaringly. Strands of her hair laced between their lips and she pushed them away with an out thrust of her tongue. A mistake. His tongue emerged to brush and taunt the soft slick of her own. She could not resist and her fingers splayed over the hard muscle of his chest.

His hand dropped from cupping her chin and slipped down to tighten about her waist. Like so many bats leaving a cave of safe haven at sundown, her senses took wild flight in every direction.

Their lips clung together, breaking, seeking, meeting, parting. Sweet goddess! What power was in his kiss. Before she'd done the kissing . . . the bewitching. She was a stranger to an honest kiss . . . a kiss free of illusion and magic . . . a kiss without a full moon's spell. A kiss that did not send her to heaven but kept her rooted to earth. Something pure and crystalline was in this kissing, not the cloying, overwhelming, drugging daze of enchantment. She felt as free and alive as the warming rays of sun upon a moor and suddenly as frightened as a fox fleeing the hounds.

Fear gripped her stomach. It was a fear of Bron mac Llyr. And then she knew . . . it was because he was real and not illusion. All encounters in her life had been with illusions . . . she had learned early on never to fully trust her eyes, her ears, or her heart. And now, before her was a man who would not disappear into the mists of magic. It was all too powerful for her and much too frightening.

She dared not love this man for he was of the same ilk as her father. She had learned that love could not long abide in a sorcerer's heart for there only the false charades and distortions of enchantment resided. She ripped herself from his arms and began moving away, shaking her head, fighting the gathering tears. Her breast heaved as she choked back the near articulation of her realization.

Beway! Beway! Bron mac Llyr. Leave now, while you can! Her mind and heart clamored.

"Milady?" Bron took a step forward. The vivacious light of his eyes registered concern and tenderness. "What is wrong? You seem afraid?"

She could not respond, her attention riveted to the storm brewing in the skies above. A sudden roll and clash of thunder pronounced the coming deluge of rain. It was as if the low rumble and rip of lightning were a foreboding message resounding, *You cannot love . . . you cannot trust.*

She threw up her arms to cover her head and ears, protecting herself as the voices of illusion echoed in reverberating thunder around her. The first drops of rain glanced off her shoulder and then mingled with her own breaking tears.

"Quickly," urged Bron, encircling her beneath his arm and hurrying her into the circle of dolmens. By the time he guided her to shelter beneath a spreading capstone she was sobbing, letting out years of long suppressed disillusionment and grief. His arms were an enfolding presence as she wept her desolation onto the leathers of his chest.

He pulled back, his hands upon the curve of her shoulders, and spoke ever so gently. "The night past we began a dance, milady . . . and I promise we shall dance and dance until the last ring of cymbal and the final clap of drum. Don't fear it. There is dark and light in us all. 'Tis about loving more than fearing. When you can do that you've won the fray."

He kissed her cheek. A kiss of honesty. And all she could think was, *Do not love . . . do not love him. In the end he will die.* But she surrendered to his embrace, she surrendered to his warmth, and she surrendered to his promise.

Chapter
6

Eyes narrowed, Sheelin glared through a casement window as Eithne and Bron mac Llyr walked below in the cashel yard. He'd seen them cross into the kitchen and later, come out again and disappear for long hours. Now, in late afternoon they reappeared more harmonious than before. On the outset, the other suitors had not been so well received by her. But then the others had been trows and tinkers . . . fools in the main.

He felt uneasy about the presence of Bron mac Llyr in his domain. That Mac Llyr was of the Tuatha de Danann, there was no doubt, and in him the powers of that formidable race had been channeled. He was a warrior and harper. But for his hand, there was no need to dress this wayfarer in the veil of illusion. Fortunately, like the others, he could not resist Eithne's beauty. Still Sheelin knew he must prepare himself to be wary and watchful. Bron mac Llyr knew of Ketha and that in itself was a danger. If he knew of Ketha then he might know something of the swan maidens of Myr. Could he be in league with them? Did he come for more than a healer? Many questions plagued Sheelin.

By the hour he was becoming more impatient to be on with his well-laid plans. Yet, it was no matter whether the harper fell in love with Eithne, only that Eithne fall in love with the harper. With the harper's head on the chopping block she would surely speak aloud to save him.

Sheelin's eyes continued to follow his daughter's movements.

In her hand, Eithne swung a basket flaring with wildflowers. Upon her head she wore a flaming garland of scarlet gila. Her silky red-gold strands tangled as wild as a briar bush. Tidiness and discipline had never been her allies. She was more comfortable with her skirts hitched up lazing on the stone stoop with the turnspits and scullions than making an appearance in the hall.

Since childhood her main pastime consisted of mucking around in the bogs or swimming in the moat. He understood her penchant for water, a trait inherited from her mother's kith. What he didn't understand was her indomitability. Her very stride sowed defiance. Why couldn't he have had an obedient daughter?

He turned away.

How long would it take? How long would she thwart him?

She was like her mother, unreasonable, with the ability to provoke beyond endurance. He had learned the hard way that swan maidens were by nature independent.

When he'd first glimpsed Ketha the sorcery of her beauty had bewitched him. Nothing filled his mind but to possess her. As time wore on, he found himself more a slave to love than he could have imagined. Even now, he felt weakened by her presence and vulnerable to her slightest demand. He did not relish a woman having that much power over him. She called forth parts of him best kept hidden. Even after all the years he'd kept her imprisoned in the tower of Woad Bog, she could still ignite in him feelings he strived to suppress. He found her strange blend of aloofness and fire irresistibly exciting, and he never tired of the challenge of conquest she represented.

At the thought of her, his desire flamed. He reached for a decanter of wine and poured a gobletful.

He'd not visited Ketha since he'd revealed his scheme of beheading Eithne's suitors as long as she refused to speak.

In a rare show of anger, Ketha had slapped him across the face, accusing, "You have no soul!"

In retrospect, he thought, *Perhaps I don't. But it matters not to me.*

He lowered himself into a deep chair and stared fixedly into a blown glass sphere balanced on a silver tower pedestal, a crystal orb of sight. The visions inside were as changeable as opals, each a miniature mirage of Myr. For now it was the nearest he could ever be to its ancient forest-cloaked hills, its meadows carpeted in wildflowers, and its transparent lakes in whose depths dwelled kingdoms beyond imagining.

Myr was an enchanted land without illusion—a realm of peace, tranquillity, and abundance. In Myr dew mysteriously digested sunlight and made it into gold. Above Myr wheeled the glimmering, star-fretted heavens, so lucid and close that the moon herself seemed to rest upon the tangled branches of great oaks. Magical beasts roamed free in Myr. White roebuck, unicorns, and rare birds with iridescent feathers gleaming with every color seen in flame. There was power in that land. Power enough to fashion whatever one needed; to bring forth mountains if one wished or call up forests if that pleased one.

He put the goblet to his lips taking a deep draught of the bloodred wine. Then he waved a dismissing hand over the glass orb—the images dissolved.

His heavy-lidded eyes slit just a trifle and a slow, quicksilver grin spread over the sharp line of his mouth. Myr was the prize he sought above all. Over the years he plotted and schemed to gather into himself various powers to serve one purpose: the ruling of this last great kingdom of old earth. No one or nothing could thwart him, not Ketha, not Eithne, nor even the swan maidens themselves.

Ketha the healer sat before the single window of her tower prison that overlooked the vast distance of the cold and lonely wild marshes. Fingers of fog reached in from the sea as the rising wind waved the tall grasses of this desolate and dreary domain. Her only companions were migrating fowl, frogs, snakes, and foraging wolves whose howls could set her shivering in the long winter nights. But for Sheelin, in all the years she'd not seen a single soul cross the shifting quagmires.

Sheelin had calculated it so. "I will give you but one window that you may anticipate my comings and mourn my goings. At last you will give me the obedience that is my due as your lord and master."

There she sat and there she would stay, a captive in the spell of Sheelin's evil. She was a prisoner in a world of sadness and shadow that mocked any longing for light and joy.

Long ago she had ceased asking, "Will he come today or will he not?" The hours, the months, and years of waiting, agonizing, had left her pale and heartsick. He came when he chose to come and she had no alternative but to accept it. She still loved Sheelin as she had always loved him, without condition, without judgment, without restraint. But how he had changed from the man she'd first met on that enchanted midsummer's eve long ago.

In those times, before he devoted his powers to the service of darkness, he sang things into being, spoke with eagles, summoned the elements. He sang songs that made the bleak heath bloom and the spirits of any who listened soar.

But no more.

He was now one of the most powerful lords of darkness in the land, and at what a price . . . he could no longer sing. He had exchanged his singer's voice for the discordant clamor of his Unseelie Court. He called forth not beauty, but evil, illusion, and devildom.

Tears collected in the corners of Ketha's eyes at the thought. Many a night as she lay alone in her tower bed, she yearned to hear once again the soul-stirring strains of Sheelin's sweet-voiced song. Yet, all she heard were the ghoulish cries of his demons rising through the marsh mists. Now, he sought to replace his own lost voice with that of Eithne's. In using the power of her swan song, he intended to invade Myr and there rule with his Unseelie Court.

Her lips pursed. She squinted and peered through the small casement window. A dark cloaked rider on a black steed carefully wended his way through the marsh.

He was coming.

After all this time Sheelin was coming to her. What had transpired at Rath Morna? Would he tell her any news? And would it be the truth? No, it would not be the truth, he rarely spoke the truth. One had to delve beneath his words. One must listen to the subtle tones of his silken voice to discover the truth.

Despite herself, her heart quickened. She hastened to change her dress and brush her hair. He had never stayed away so long before. Last time when they had fought, she had told him never to return. She had held his brackish gaze and vowed that she would rather die than see him again. But in her heart's depths she knew she would die if she did not see him. To love too well was at the core of every swan maiden's being. It was the warp and weft she had woven the moment she touched eyes with him. The seeress, Bree, had warned her to guard her heart, but Ketha could not stop her heart from loving him.

In the beginning, he'd been honorable and honest, truly an awakened soul.

What had happened?

Over and over in her mind she had retraced the events that had transformed him.

When she and Sheelin came upon Rath Morna it had been abandoned. She had never wished to stay more than a night, but he had insisted. She had found him studying crumbling parchment scrolls until dawn. The days passed, servants began appearing and more. As if overnight, elegant furnishings filled the halls and rooms. Soon banquets were spread. Strangers danced and feasted in the hall.

"Who are these people?" she would ask Sheelin. "I know none of them."

"Only travelers I have invited in. We are wealthy now," he would declare, avoiding her gaze.

Her renown as a healer spread over the land and often those who came, came not for Sheelin's lavish hospitality but for her own healing touch.

Sheelin watched and questioned her. "What magics, what spells do you chant? What is the source of this power?"

"I do not know. I chant no spells or call upon no magic but the magic of goodness. I know only that the healing touch is a gift from the goddess to my kind."

After a time, upon Sheelin's orders, any pilgrims seeking healing from Ketha were turned away at the gates. When she had confronted him, he replied, "You are too great a lady to soil your hands on the vermin infested peasants that seek a free healing."

But Ketha knew better.

Sadly, she knew Sheelin was jealous of her gift. In all his dark undertakings, nothing compared to the healing touch. His jealousy fomented and emerged in other ways.

When Eithne was born he discovered she had inherited the singer's voice. The voice he had bartered to the powers of darkness. Not only could she sing, but in her childhood innocence, her song could undo his own evil magics. She sang his rich tapestries into tatters and hummed his feasts into crumbs. Upon the eve of Eithne's tenth rebirth day, Ketha learned that Sheelin plotted to steal Eithne's voice.

In the dead of night, she took her daughter and together they fled Rath Morna pursued by the demons of Sheelin's Unseelie Court. Once captured, in the face of Sheelin's wrath, Ketha forbade Eithne to speak on threat of Sheelin's stealing her voice. In that moment, Ketha learned one did not cross Sheelin for retribution would be most certain. He imprisoned her in Woad Bog Tower. He wrapped the tower in a cloak of invisibility where he alone could enter.

Ketha breathed a deep-felt sigh . . . and gathered her hair into a netting of rubies.

In those first months, she had wept and moaned. She had begged piteously for her freedom but Sheelin did not relent. After all the years she had made her peace with loneliness. She spent her days sewing an intricate cloak of feathers. The feathers were gifts from her kindred winged-ones, blown to her on the invisible wind to the ledge of her invisible lancet window. Many had heard of the disappearance of Ketha, the swan healer, as they migrated through the wild marshes, but not even the sharp eye of an eagle could penetrate Sheelin's magics.

"Ketha."

Ketha turned. She had not quite finished tying the bodice lacings of her gown. Sheelin stood before her, his entry as stealthy as a fox.

She felt dissected by his incredibly deep steady gaze. It was always so. He could probe the very depths of her heart, mind, and body. A part of her wanted to run into his arms and again feel the warmth of human touch. But pride kept her rooted in a demeanor of royal dignity. And always in the back of her mind was the hope that perhaps the old Sheelin had returned. The man who was warm, ever generous and friendly, despite his commanding airs. She searched his flawless features from the obsidian eyes to the ignoble turn of his lips.

How could she still love this man? He had betrayed her, deceived her, and imprisoned her. How?

He stepped toward her. His forefinger traced lightly over her chin, down the curve of her throat to rest on the swell of her breast. His touch burned. It always burned, but oh such a sweet burning. His dark sorcery called her own darkness. No matter how aloof she may pretend to be, she could not resist him. He knew she could not.

"Ketha." His tone was a caressing of her name. "Love me. The moon shines full this night."

He knew no swan sister could deny her lover under a luminous moon.

"I have missed you, Ketha. I am in need of healing. Can you heal my wicked heart? Can you mend my broken soul with your healer's touch? Do try, my beloved."

He kissed her cheek, her brow, her lips. Somehow Ketha knew she might kiss ten thousand men and never would she taste such fire. She shrugged off his hands.

"You must heal your own wicked heart, my lord Sheelin." She stepped away, full knowing he would follow and she would relent. Sheelin had to win. He would risk anything to win short of his own life, and he might even risk that.

"And is my heart so wicked?" He stepped near, his lips touched lightly the nape of her neck. "I can still love you." His words fell like sparks on the glittering mesh of her hair.

She whirled to face him. "You do not love me, you possess me. There is a great difference."

"Come to me . . . that we might explore this difference."

"Will you never tire of this game you play?" she said, a tremble in her voice.

"You burn for me as much as I burn for you."

"I burn as one in hell. This tower where you imprison me is my netherworld."

"Ketha, Ketha . . . " Like a beguiling serpent's embrace he coiled his arms around her and lowered his mouth to hers.

She stood still as stone, but her own being was molten with desire for him. Her lips responded with the desperateness of loneliness.

* * *

Rose and golden, dawn came to the marshes spreading over the rim of the horizon, touching reed and bird wing alike with the light of awakening. Rays of sunlight flowed through the small lancet window dappling the down coverings of Ketha's great oak pillared bed. She reached over and laid her hand on Sheelin's chest. She gazed at his sleeping face and knew he was a stranger to her. Tears of sadness trickled from the corners of her eyes. In the past years she always wept after making love with him because she felt the incompleteness, the holding back on his part, and his inability to surrender.

Aye, he had lust and passion, but no love . . . no vulnerability. He could risk all else but his heart. Softly, she began to hum.

He blinked, his features cloudy with the incoherence of waking.

"Stop!" The sharpness of his voice silenced Ketha as surely as if he held a dagger to her throat.

"I have commanded you never, never to sing in my presence." He thrust her hand off him and sat up.

She lay there feeling the burn of his censure. She stared at his bare muscled back. The urge was overwhelming to throw herself against him, to weep, to beg him to become again the Sheelin she'd fallen in love with years before. But it would do no good, he had barricaded himself away.

She drew herself up and on her knees moved behind him. She pushed the tangle of her red hair aside and leaning into him she wrapped her arms around him. He felt cold. She might have as easily embraced a statue.

She whispered, "Who are you?"

There was a tangible quiet in the room. He seemed to almost have stopped breathing. Then he spoke, "I am whoever I choose to be."

"And who do you choose to be?"

"I choose, dear lady, to be the ruler of Myr."

He said this with such cold force that a sickening feeling engulfed her. "No one rules Myr."

Shrugging her off, he shifted and climbed out of the bed. His arrogant indifference made her shiver.

Imperiously, his black eyes met hers and he said, "I will!"

And in that instant she had no doubt that he would. She stared at him, all her emotion concealed. But within her outrage boiled. She knew that Eithne was the only bastion between Sheelin and Myr. She watched him begin to dress, and in her mind brewed her own stratagems.

"How many suitors have you beheaded?" she asked forthrightly, drawing beneath the warmth of the covers.

He looked up from lacing his boots. "Twelve!"

"She will never speak. You waste your time."

"I think not. One has come . . . a sea clansman of the Tuatha de Danann. He will win her heart. I foresee it."

"And if he doesn't?"

He straightened and walked over to her. His large hand reached out ruthlessly capturing the circle of her neck. He pulled her toward him. His hostile stare penetrated her own. The darkness of him frightened her. "It will be your own neck on the chopping block. I don't know why I did not think of it sooner."

"She will not speak, even to save my life."

"You underestimate the power of love, Ketha."

"And what do you know of love? A man who puts ambition above all."

His fingers released her throat and entangled within the soft filaments of her hair, dragging her face to him until his lips hovered above her own. "I know enough to keep you burning for me. I know enough that when I leave, you weep. I know enough, Ketha . . ." He covered her lips in a moist kiss that sent flame ripping through her body.

She twisted away her head and pushed him off. "You know nothing of love, Sheelin," she spat out. "Nothing! You know of lust and darkness and usury. Leave me! Leave me!" she screamed from her very depths.

She buried her face in the pillows and wept.

It may have been hours or only minutes, but when at last she lifted her head and wiped the curtain of tears from her cheeks, Sheelin was gone.

How she hated him! How she loved him!

7

Footsteps broke the silence of the night. Eithne's heart quickened a single beat. Her eyes left her own reflection in the gilt frame looking glass and riveted to her chamber door.

She listened.

A muted knock came. She did not immediately rise to her feet; instead she continued to sit on the velvet tufted stool and stare at her reflection. She frowned— if only she were as beautiful as the illusions of Sheelin's court. She caught her lower lip between her teeth and ruminated over how she might remedy her appearance with magic. Her mother had taught her the rules of white magic. Use it honestly . . . and never do harm.

Slowly, she fanned open her right hand and with her fingertips touched her forehead's reflection on the glass . . . a golden circlet appeared on the crown of her head. She touched the hollow of her throat and a choker of emeralds magically graced her long neck. Her hand moved to her breast and suddenly her rough spun gunna transformed into a fall of holly green silk which pooled about her slippered feet.

Louder, the knock sounded again.

Her nerves thrumming, Eithne rose and walked to the door. Her hand trembled as she reached for the great ring latch. The first night she had begged the sea clansman to stay and he had left. The second night she had called him, but feared his coming. Tonight she no longer feared him.

As Eithne pulled the door open, the hinges groaned like an old woman asked to fall upon her knees.

The figure that met Eithne was a surprise. She blinked once to be sure it was he. How grand he appeared. She guessed he must have availed himself of his own magics.

Her inspection roamed from his jeweled turban hat offset by his lengthy black hair, to the satin blue shimmer of his intricately embroidered cloak. A gold filigree belt slouched about his narrow hips and black silk leggings outlined the muscular shape of his long legs. He drew up, removed his hat, and in a flowing gesture graced her with a half bow, straightened and tossed his cloak rakishly over one broad shoulder.

"Milady." Though his lips posed solemnly, his face relaxed with warmth and greeting.

She tilted her own head in a shy welcome.

Yet, out of nervousness she held back. She withheld her smile. She withheld words she might have spoken if she could speak, and she withheld her heart.

What she could not withhold was her need for him, her yearning, her longing for his touch that so consoled and comforted.

He stepped toward her and she opened her arms to him. She felt the largeness of him fill the expanse of her embrace as his own arms encircled her. He pressed her close, her cheek rested on the soft silk of his tunic. The heat of him burned through, caressing her skin like starshine dusts the moon. His heart pulse murmured deep rhythms to her own. How could she have lived so long and never known that touch and nearness could be so restoring?

The last safe haven in her life had been in her mother's arms, years ago. Eithne could still remember being dragged away, crying and calling for Ketha. The wave of memory caused her to tighten her arms around Bron as if he too would be torn from her. Even so, in this moment he seemed content enough to be her mainstay. Through the morning storm, within the cover of the stones he had comforted her . . . kissed her cheek and hair. No one had done such a thing to her that she could remember.

Gibbers would be aghast if he knew that someone kissed the "ugly, evil gurrul" and did not break out in a plague of warts. She peeked just to be sure Bron was not showing speckles upon his face.

His skin was clear. She sighed with relief and nuzzled her cheek again to his broad chest.

He stroked her hair and whispered, "I am content to hold you here, but I think it best you allow me to step inside or word will go to your father that I have not gained entrance into your chamber."

Reluctantly, she released him. His arm kept a protective loop over her shoulders as he moved inside. After a strangled creak, the door cannoned shut.

Bron jumped slightly. "It appears I am again your willing prisoner for this night, milady. I am ready to partake of your hospitality."

Eithne followed his encompassing gaze as it traveled the expanse of her barren chamber. Except for the window seat and one velvet stool there were no chairs. Her bed was a down stuffed pallet before the flameless hearth. Her toilette and wardrobe were secreted behind a homespun curtain in one corner. But for the gilt looking glass it was a pauper's haven in comparison to the rest of Rath Morna. She chose it so. Her room remained a sanctuary free of her father's illusion.

I have none to offer, she enlightened.

He looked down at her. "You hedge. No more shape-shifting?"

She smiled. *After last night I have learned my lesson.*

"Nevertheless, you are to fulfill my every wish. What did you with the others?"

I did what I chose to do. I will not tell you for there would be no surprises.

He chuckled. "You speak like your gillie troll . . . the keeper of secrets. I would have no secrets between you and me, Lady Eithne. Mayhap that is my first wish."

Then it may be your last. Rath Morna is the domain of secrets . . . dark secrets. She could play this game. Like most, he liked to know secrets as well as keep secrets. She sensed he could be adept at pulling secrets out of others and locking his own against all questions.

"But still it is my wish," he insisted.

And how many wishes must I fulfill in seven nights?

"Now, you are the skeleton at the feast. Can you promise it will end at just seven?"

She pursed her lips evasively. *I cannot promise.*

"Then what can you promise?"

I do not make promises, because I might have to break them. No one should make promises or swear on things for the sensible reason that no one can predict with certainty what might happen. Promises are for those who like to fool themselves, and others, into thinking they are in control of their own future.

"Ah . . ." His eyes lightened with appreciation. "'Tis a fair philosopher you are. And if the future is so unsure then let us not waste our time together. Bring on the wine and dancing girls."

I cannot. There is no wine and only one dancing girl.

"Is it too late for me to leave? I have been duped unless you have some better pastime." She did not miss the expectancy in his voice.

She wanted to please him. She hadn't wanted to please anyone for a long, long time. She would forget the circumstances and pretend, just for tonight. Well, maybe tomorrow night too.

She smiled mischievously. *I do. Come sit down.*

Bron searched for a chair and finally chose the window seat. He removed his hat and in a deft swirl, his cape. He arranged his long, loose-limbed body comfortably on the stone seat while looking at her with those sincere, serious, made-to-melt-the-coldest-heart eyes.

Inwardly, Eithne vowed not to melt. She pulled up the stool and sat at his feet.

You must close your eyes, she commanded so she could keep her concentration.

"I'm not so trustworthy. Might I keep but one eye cracked?"

She reached up and covered his eyes with one hand. *Nay, it will spoil the wishing. Isn't it enough that this night you can have your heart's desire?*

"I do not have a heart's desire, milady. There is no profit in it for once attained what is the point of living?"

Eithne was taken aback. What philosophy was this? Only a knight of the road would think it. She tried again. *Then what is your wish?*

"I have told you. I wish no secrets between us. I wish you to always speak true."

That would be very hard for me because I do not speak at all.

A low chuckle rumbled in his throat. "Then that is my wish." He removed her hand from his eyes and turned the palm upward. His own fingers caressed hers softly, and she felt explosion in his touch.

His sea-watching gaze delved her own for an intense moment. "I would have you speak . . . speak my name and call me to your arms . . . to your bed . . . to your heart. In passion's heat I would have you cry for me aloud . . . and beg my blade to find sweet haven in your sheath."

Eithne's eyes widened and she swallowed back her disquiet. Unleashed passion was not her wont. This night she needed her hand held, her nose kissed, and her ears filled with gentle poems. She drew her hand away. This man was not safe. The others she could handle, but him . . . He disarmed her with his forth-right demands . . . his desires.

She thought to confess that it would be he who cried aloud. For when his blade did first enter her sheath he'd feel passion's fire, truly. For it was the way with a swan maiden that the first man to cross the threshold of her virginity paid a price of pain.

She gathered herself and her lips firmed. *You ask too much and more. I cannot grant this wish . . . is there no other?*

He dropped his hand to his knee and shrugged with a half-disappointed laugh. "Arrah. A lad must dream, milady."

Leave off dreaming and forget the wishing.

"Is it not the same?"

No, I do not think so. With dreams you can do your own spinning, while wishes . . . wishes are granted by another . . . or by providence.

"Hummm . . . Mayhap I am too slothful this night to do my own dream spinning. So what is left?"

Magic.

"And who will pay the price of the magic? Magic does not come free."

I will. Her mind was resigned. Had she not paid the price of magic all her life? The "wicked gurrul" could pay one time more.

"Are you sure?" His voice was wary.

I am sure as heather on the heath—

". . . And mud in the bog," he finished, his own features lightening.

What first?

He pursed his lips. "Humph. I think I would have a

silk pillow to cushion this cold seat . . . and a fire in your hearth . . . and"—he touched her hair just above her ear—"a white rose in your hair."

The words had barely passed his lips when all appeared. A silken pillow, a flaming fire, and . . . Eithne reached to discover a fragrant rose against her cheek. Her delight was only surpassed by her surprise. He could be safe after all . . . the night would not be lost.

But now it will be you who pays the price of magic, she protested.

"Aye, but what have I to lose?" he said, amused. "We will share the magic and the cost. Agreed?"

Eithne studied his face and saw mischief there. She would not resist . . . she could not.

Agreed.

"Then it is your turn, milady. What wondrous pleasures can you conjure?" he challenged.

She rubbed her hands together with anticipation. *You must close your eyes.*

"I fear you will make me vanish," said Bron, remembering Coup's warning that he should not close his eyes in her presence.

Nay, I will not. At least not yet.

"Then you will vanish."

Eithne's inward mirth nearly erupted in a giggle. *For certain I will vanish, but only until you open your eyes again.*

Risking, he closed his eyes and grinned, a bit sheepishly. "Arrah. Do your deed and be hasty . . . the night will soon pass."

Like a breaking wave, the deep fragrance of flowers

crested and saturated Bron's senses. He could not only smell the air of high summer, but he heard the lilting trickle of water.

Not yet. He received Eithne's clear caution as she sensed his impatience. Suddenly something alighted on his head and he heard the lulling coo of a dove . . . then a nightingale trilled sweetly in answer. Had he been conveyed out-of-doors? Daringly, he slit one eye.

You may not peek! scolded Eithne.

Too late! He opened wide his eyes. His jaw fell askance.

The rare, the exotic filled the expanse of his vision. Above on lattice bowers drooped purple wisteria, while rose and woodbine entwined over the door and hearth. In room center, fern and tall-topped plumes thick with flowers encircled a flowing fountain. Candlelit lanterns hung about, casting an ephemeral glow. In all his travels, he'd not seen the like of it.

He shooed the dove off his shoulder and came to his feet with the intent of walking over to the fountain. There, water sprayed from the beak of a sculptured swan like flying diamonds. She was quite the magician herself.

No. No. Eithne pointed to his boots.

He saw the floor was strewn with rose petals, lavender buds, and sweet violets.

"You want me to take off my boots?"

Aye, indeed . . . you must experience the whole of it. And more is to come.

"What more? 'Tis already beyond my humble imaginings."

We will commune . . .

"And . . . ?" Bron prompted hopefully.

And you can speak sweet poetry.

"But I am no poet."

You are a harper . . . of some renown.

"How do you know this?"

Gibbers. For the right bribe he tells me all.

"And what is the right bribe that I might avail myself of his secrets?"

I'll not tell. You must discover his weakness for yourself.

"Hummm . . . And what is your weakness?"

'Tis surely not nosy harpers.

He laughed, deeply. "Then, milady, if you wish my boots off then I ask you to help me remove them."

Remove your own boots with your own magic. I do draw the line. I'm no peasant maid here to do menial bidding. Would you ask a castle builder to cook a Lammas Day cake?

"Arrah. You make your point. But I am a simple man and need no magic to remove my boots . . . only the courteous use of a fair lady's backside as leverage."

Beway! There is nothing simple about you. You insult me. You'd have me on my knees lapping rose petals. 'Tis much ado over taking off a pair of boots. Her lips twisted begrudgingly.

Facing him she bent down, took firm hold of his boot, and pulled mightily. Off it slipped. The other came off just as slickly. *'Tis done! milord. Next time do it yourself, now you've seen how.*

Her head turned about. She sniffed the air and fanned it with her hand. *When last did you remove your boots? 'Tis a fine effort I've made to scent this room. Now all seems lost. I will say it spoils the magic . . . and the sweet air of communion. I had such plans. . . .*

"I'll bet you did," Bron said a bit mockingly. "Forgive me, milady. I fear the real tarnishes the unreal. 'Tis the lesson of life. Mayhap I should return to the stable and you find yourself a suitor without flaw."

No!

He felt, not heard the initial vehemence of her answer.

She clutched his arm. *No. 'Tis not my wish to find the perfect knight in polished armor. My father's court abounds with such as those. I seek for what is beneath the illusion.*

Bron studied her intently, deciding whether she was real or not. Could an illusion be so honest? She fascinated him and he enjoyed the mystery of wondering.

He covered her hand with his own. "Then dismiss your night's magic and lie in my arms without your false facades and fragrances. I will speak to you poetry, but poetry of my desire. We will commune . . . the communion of lust."

The mark of her dismay was in her eyes and they had the glaze of being lost.

I cannot.

And with those two words he knew she could not.

He would no longer press it. He rose to his feet, keeping her hand within his.

"Mayhap I can make amends by washing my feet in the fountain."

She smiled then and her eyes shone with vast relief. Aye, he thought, full-flesh intimacy would expose her as illusion . . . but then again maybe not. This was the challenge to unfold.

There was something of the waif in her as well as the firebrand. He was beginning to understand that when she laughed she might be sobbing inwardly and when she cried, she was inwardly joyous. Nevertheless, he would flow with the night's magic. Alas, for carnal desire. Tonight he would be monk, not lover.

He seated himself on the fountain edge and rolled up his leggings to the knee. When he dipped his feet into the water a warm tingling rushed through him, refreshing and relaxing him.

Lifting her skirts to display her shapely thighs, Eithne sat down beside him and lowered her own legs into the water. He must get used to her duality, the one aspect that announced wantonness and the other that denied it. Mayhap it was the fault of Sheelin's sorcery . . . with the intent to better torment her suitors,

Do you have a philosophy of love, milord?

Her question was unexpected, one he could not directly answer. He watched an iridescent winged dragonfly sail past within inches of his nose. Somewhere in a dusty corner of his mind he remembered his father telling him that love was as illusory as a dragonfly's wings and that it was never completely as it seemed. He snatched at a red blossom floating in the pool and twirled it in his fingers.

Sheelin says love is an opiate. Gibbers says love is a fool's folly.

"Do you believe them?"

I don't know what to believe.

Bron leaned over and tucked the flower behind Eithne's ear and said, "Believe everything and nothing. Be aware that Gibbers has never loved and Sheelin . . . Aye, love does not serve dark sorcery . . . though it is the ultimate sorcery itself. You should have asked someone who knew something about love."

That is why I am asking you. She gave him the full force of her soft luminous eyes. The rainbow of colors spiraled like rare opals.

"What makes you think I know any more than Sheelin and Gibbers?"

Because you have loved.

"How do you know this?"

You have a soul. Those with souls, love.

Bron smiled reluctantly. "Not always. I have a missing hand to prove it. Arrah, love . . . true love is a rare find."

And what is "true" love?

Bron caught another flower from the pool. "I'm not so sure. I'm still looking. But I can tell you there are many kinds of love."

She gave him her full attention. *What kinds?*

"One kind catches you unaware like the flash of gold in sunlight. Another starts out comfortably and wears through the years like a good pair of boots. Some kind of love is fanciful, illusory, like this. . . ." He waved his hand in the air to include the whole of their surroundings. "'Tis poetry, song, communion, and sentimentality. It is like the enchanted kiss you honored me with the night of my arrival. It can carry you to heaven and beyond. This is the safest kind of love."

And what is the most dangerous?

"Arrah, now that is true love."

But why?

"Because, milady Eithne, true love hurts. True love is risk taking. It can be spit and venom. You can be cast off, betrayed, and exposed. It can rend your heart in two."

Why would anyone seek such a thing?

"You don't seek it . . . it finds you."

She grimaced. *Beway, I hope it doesn't find me. I'm content with fanciful love.* She pulled her feet from the pool and turned about. Wiping her own legs with a silken scarf, she continued, *Does nothing good come of true love?*

"All and everything."

The gaze she turned on Bron was one of bafflement. He shrugged. "'Tis one of life's great riddles."

She rested her hands in her lap. *Now I am very curious. You must tell me of the women you have loved, Bron mac Llyr.*

Bron managed to appear perfectly composed, even amused, but he was not sure that telling one woman about other women in his life was wise.

At his hesitation she prompted, *You have loved,*

haven't you? Not true love, but the other sort you spoke of.

He had lifted his own feet from the fountain. She leaned nearer and began wiping off the beading water that trickled in rivulets down his muscular calves. He was warmed by her attention. She did not stop with drying, but placed one of his feet upon the cradle of her lap. Pouring oil from a delicate glass beaker into the palm of her hand she began slowly and tenderly to massage his foot.

He was content to close his eyes and revel in the experience of her touch until she prompted once more, *You must answer or I shall stop my ministerings.*

"Nay, do not! I shall speak until dawn if need be. But let us move to a more comfortable place." He had not finished speaking before a silk pillowed pallet appeared beneath the greenery bower. Even more quickly he was on his feet and sweeping her into his arms.

Her surprise was upon her face. She caught the glass beaker in her hand just as he stepped across the crush of petals on the floor. Carefully, he set her down and arranged himself against the pillows. Cross-legged she sat opposite him, adjusted herself, and took his foot in hand.

Now speak.

The corner of his eyes played with a smile. "I've had so many loves, where shall I begin?"

She was not smiling. In truth her lips seemed fairly crimped. *At the beginning. The first. If you can remember that far back.*

For Bron the act of love had always been a feast of

the senses. He had put little heart into it. There had never been the need or demand for it. He'd never waylaid long enough with one woman in one place. So of the fair faces that circled through his mind only that of Sarenn remained vivid.

"I will confess that 'tis a rare man who forgets his first love. Mine was not only unforgettable but unforgivable. I was but fifteen summers old when I was out fishing off the rookery of Glynmere Isle. 'Tis somewhat of an enchanted place. I had been warned, but was young and bold and seeking adventure. A mermaid came up out of the sea as playful as a dolphin. Her hair was spun gold and her eyes . . ."

He paused and looked at Eithne appreciatively.

"But for your own eyes, Lady Eithne, I have not seen the like. Her song was sweet and cajoling . . . her bare, full breasts bobbed in the sea like ripe fruit prime for plucking. But 'twas I that was plucked. She lured me into the sea. I followed her down into her watery kingdom."

And why did you not drown? Eithne asked with curiosity.

"I was enchanted. You yourself know such arts."

I suppose I do. But not that particular one, she added, as though it were worthy of her study.

"She was a sea nymph. She taught me of love and the ways of the sea kingdoms. Time lost meaning . . ." His voice faded as he fell into momentary reverie.

And?

His gaze focused on Eithne. "And then my father came and rescued me. I was so smitten by her charms I raised my own sword against him. The instant my sword struck his, the enchantment was broken. 'Twas his own skill in sorcery that saved us both from drowning."

Completing her task, Eithne released his foot and moved beside him. *What became of the sea nymph?*

Bron did not miss the opportunity to loop his arm around her shoulders. She rested her head against him and he toyed with the copper strands idly.

"She remained in her sea kingdom. I did see her again but was never so foolish as to leap into the sea after her. If I were to choose one woman I have loved, it would be her."

Then why did you not handfast with her?

"I could not. She is not of my kith. My children would have scales and fins."

Unexpectedly, Eithne shifted, drawing her toes beneath her gown. Bron did not miss the significance of it. He had spoken thoughtlessly.

He continued to hold her as if holding her would erase the blunder. Yet something else was happening between them. He discovered it was easy to sit in silence with her. To open his mind and accept the communion of her thoughts. In the ensuing quiet, he felt a relationship building based on mutual necessity, physical proximity, and irresistible attraction.

I would love to live by the sea. 'Tis a wish of mine.

"Arrah. You've missed life itself, but only if you've an affinity with water. Mayhap you are a land-lover bred."

I am that, but the sea has always called me. When I fl—go to the marshes and look beyond to the sea I feel such longing. Do you live in a rath?

"Nay, there is no need for fortress walls. I live on an island. The sea is our moat."

Is it beautiful?

"If stone is beautiful. Aye 'tis beautiful."

'Tis an islet of stone?

"Naught but stone . . . and sea." He nestled his nose in the concave behind her earlobe and inhaled lightly. "We all carry the ocean within us. You smell and taste of ocean. Tears taste of the sea and the blood that flows in your veins mirrors the tides. Did you know that?"

She turned her face to him and his lips slipped across her cheek . . . the brush of his lips over her mouth startled open her half-closed eyelids. He made another tentative pass, feather light. The taste of her lips held a cinnamonlike tingle. His own eyes open, he gazed into hers. They swirled like eddying pools of bewitchment.

The lantern light shone like hidden stars in the mass of her curls, and he pushed the locks aside to expose the ivory softness of her graceful neck. His fingers whispered over her shoulder, caressing the smooth round. His own heart pace quickened and his throat tightened. A mortal woman could not match her beauty. He feared he was falling in love with an illusion.

He would tease her until she responded. Kissing was a form of communion and if her pursuit be communion the night long he would commune. His lips trailed down the warm arch of her throat to halt at the icy emerald choker. He dared go no lower.

He halted and looked straight into her opalescent

eyes to assess the waters. She gave him a round-eyed gaze that held every promise he could dream. She leaned to him and him to her. Together their lips met in a pleasure bonding of sweet reunion . . . and again the burst of cinnamon filled his senses.

He buried his face against the fragrant skin of her neck, feeling the drowsy course of her pulse.

Then he felt a wild dizziness.

He was standing beside her in a copse, a little clearing in a wood. More magic, he thought. She was dressed in green velvet, her copper hair cascaded down her back to brush the ground. In her hands she held a large earthen chalice that was covered with moss and delicate flowers.

"I have something for you," she spoke aloud, her voice sweetly crystalline.

He seemed unable to find his own voice to speak. She lifted up the chalice. He took the coolness of it in hand and drank. He knew he was drinking love . . . pure love.

Light and color swirled around him. For a moment his awareness spiraled outward until it interlaced with the essence of Eithne. She stretched out her hands. He returned the chalice to her and she drank as well.

Around him, everything seemed shining. Eithne placed the chalice on a stone altar. She turned to him and showered upon him a gaze of voluminous love. He'd never experienced such opening, such overflowing, such radiance pouring from someone's countenance.

He felt power rising within him like a great sea

swell. He reached for her hand and brought it to his lips, turned it, and kissed the palm.

He opened his mouth to tell her that she was very beautiful, but he made no sound. Even so, between them was such an open knowingness that he knew she understood his thoughts without speaking them. He soul-gazed into the diamond clarity of her eyes and felt an incredible lightness of being . . . an incredible joy as if after a long, lonely journey he'd come home. He opened his arms to her and she stepped into his embrace. Aye, he thought . . . We've begun a dance and what a dance it is.

Chapter

Bron awoke before dawn, a wassailer in the ashes of magic. He lay in darkness, cold, and intemperance. Awareness came slowly. He remained in Eithne's chambers, upon Eithne's pallet, without Eithne. The forest . . . the drinking of pure love from the chalice in her hands, had all been a dream.

He groaned. The bite of cinnamon clung to his lips. He realized she had drugged him with a sleeping potion. Aye, those lips! She had smeared it upon her own lips. He could not feel too sorry for himself. He'd been warned by Coup of her bewitchments. Clearly, he'd not yet won her trust.

Still bedazed he sat up and reached with his sword hand to scratch his face. The linen wrapped stub met the grating texture of his unshaven beard.

"Arrah!" he grumbled aloud. "That's what comes of believing the illusion." He'd allowed himself that perverse pleasure and now in the aftermath, he paid. He felt atrocious, used, and heart-bruised. He managed to stand up and walk over to the window.

Moonlight filtered in. He deeply breathed in the crisp air. His head ached, his mouth tasted bad, and he couldn't clearly focus. He sat down upon the seat internally chastising himself for not being more canny.

Where had she gone, he wondered? Mayhap she vanished with the rest of the illusion, he thought sourly. Then his fingers touched something on the stone window seat. He picked it up and held it in the moonlight. It was a white long wing feather. A swan feather!

Just as quickly, everything connected in his mind. The webbing between her toes, her quicksilver eyes, and her netherworld aura. Eithne was a swan maiden! The realization lifted the miasma of his spirit. She was not an illusion. He felt great relief at this discovery as if a weighty burden had been dropped not only from his shoulders, but from his heart as well.

Aye, still she was a swan witch and not of his kith . . . but there was kith and then there was kith. The swan sisters of Myr were legendary for their beauty, wisdom, and healing gifts. The rare man who was chosen by one as mate was counted fortunate indeed.

So, he continued ruminating, if Eithne was Sheelin's true daughter then her mother was a swan maiden. And with that awareness, the purpose of his journey became forefront again. Through Eithne, he would find Ketha, the swan healer.

A shadow crossed the face of the moon. He saw the lowering, spread wing spiral of an alabaster swan glide over cashel walls.

She was returning.

He paused, captivated by her form and grace as swan. The tradition of his sea clan held the swan sacred and the courier of transformation. He smiled to himself, thinking that since the first moment he saw her, he'd had nothing but transformation in his life . . . and not all of it was good.

With haste, he went back to lie upon the pallet to pretend sleep. For the time being, she must not know he knew. Aye, there were many secrets at Rath Morna and he intended to unmask them all.

Eithne transformed from swan to maid as she passed through the window casement. The transition left her momentarily unsteady on her feet and slightly disoriented. Thank the goddess! Mac Llyr was where she had left him, sleeping soundly. She wondered what visions filled his head. Surely, he'd sleep until sunrise from the potion. She stepped over the dried crush of wilted rose petals and slipped down beside him. Her night flight had left her chilled and she snuggled closer to him for warmth.

A soft, pleasurable mumble sounded in his chest. He turned toward her spoon fashion and coiled his arm around her waist. His nearness was like a smoldering hearth. She relaxed against him. She might have been wrong to give him the sleeping potion, but still she could not trust him.

Again her search had been fruitless. Where was Ketha? Could she even be within these cashel walls? In her mind, Eithne ran over and over the places Sheelin might have imprisoned her. Had she missed exploring one dark passage in the maze of the dungeons below? She could worm nothing out of Gibbers, and if anyone knew, it would be him.

Ketha had always told her, "There is another world. It is hidden in this one."

Night after night she had flown above forest and heath, only to return to Rath Morna in despair. By his spells and magics, Sheelin entrapped her mother and herself in his dark web of power. Someday she would find the portal into that other world of Myr and reunite with the swan sisters. Yet, her fear was that Sheelin would follow. Until she found Ketha, she had no recourse but to remain at Rath Morna.

She glanced over at the sleeping form of Bron mac Llyr. Even he was no true, safe haven. He himself could fall victim to Sheelin's evil. Tears glazed Eithne's eyes and hopelessness permeated her heart. In the glow of magic she had taken comfort in Bron's proximity. She had dreamed a wee dream that he might take her to his isle in the sea, but 'twas only a dream and had no more substance than the evening past.

Her fingers shifted, brushing against his own. His were slender and shapely, with strong nails that suggested an agile strength. Harper's fingers. She would like to hear him play, but with a severed hand he could play little more than what a curious child might pluck in mischief. Sadly, she would never hear him play his harp. She would never see his homeland in the sea and she would never escape the darkness of Rath Morna. Grief welled up inside her, grief for what could never be.

The moon set and soon dawn would break. Her chambers seemed a black dungeon in which shadows danced like tormented souls. As she lay there she sank deeper and deeper into misery. She knew her misery was the toll she paid for the night's magic, but knowing did not ease the pain of her suffering.

When the first rays of sunlight splayed across the walls, Eithne turned to see if Bron still slept. Her scrutiny followed the hard bones of his face to the black brows and even blacker hair. He looked dissipated. He was unshaven and bearing out scruffiness. The night past he'd appeared much grander, but now, oddly she found him unappealing. The cloying sweet scents were gone. He smelled musky . . . ambery, and, aye, cinnamony.

A sudden, she concluded she was lying beside the biggest mistake of her life. How could she have ever allowed him to kiss her at all or imagined she might commune with the like of him?

She peered hard at him. His eyelids flashed open . . . startling her.

"You'll not be kissing me back to fairy. I've had my fill for the time being. 'Tis worse than an endless winter's debauchery." Groaning, he rolled over and ran his hand through his disheveled hair. "Arrah! I've paid twice in one night for the magic. I'll not pay again. Oh, fair maiden, keep thine enchanted lips to thy self."

Offended, Eithne sat up. In truth the sparkle had worn off. Her chamber was in tatters and so was her mood. He might be more appealing in morning light, but he was not so gallant to spurn her kiss. She could

SWAN WITCH

not help it. Her eyes began to tear. What ever did she
see in him? She sniffled her dismay and made to stand.

"While you're on your feet, I'll have a basin of water
to wash off my lips." His voice was brittle and
commanding.

She felt the heat of temper rising. *I'm no menial to
do your bidding.*

"'Tis the bargain. You were not so fleering the night
past. I fall asleep with an angel and awaken to a
banshee."

You be a spriggan yourself! Vexed, she crossed the
room to fetch the washbasin from her dressing corner.
She tapped loose the thin crust of ice. As she returned,
the water sloshed like a storm tossed sea over the
basin's edges. She stopped before him and held it out
for him to take.

He made no effort in that regard. "Now you are
here, I'll have you wash that foul potion off my lips
yourself."

*Begobs, you could not take off your own boots. Now,
you cannot wipe off your own mouth. 'Tis feeble you
are and 'tis soon you'll be about the land, a one-handed
beggar.*

It was cruel to say, and oddly she felt no remorse.
Bron's eyes fired with anger. Standing, he thrust his
hand before her face. It was a perfect hand in the
illusion.

"Leave off! Or this one-handed beggar will box your
ears and you'll be deaf as well as mute."

Her lips curled in a sneer. She was not so docile as
to stand there and take his threats. Abruptly, she
tipped the basin over his head.

"Arra-a-a-h!" he sputtered leaping away.

The spectacle of him cursing and wheezing caused Eithne great satisfaction, but only up to the instant his fingers clutched her neck and an involuntary whimper tore from her throat.

Panic filled her. Now he was like the others. Where was the warmth of touch and sensitivity of nature? The sickening dread that he too had become corrupted by the darkness of Rath Morna jangled her awareness.

His grip only lasted for a heartbeat. A shift passed over his visage more felt than seen. He left her and strode across the room, picked up the water pitcher, and came toward her.

Too late! Eithne dashed for cover.

He did not throw the crockery at her, but the water. The bite of the icy water upon her face was like an awakening slap. Aghast, she stood breathless and dripping.

Without taking his eyes from her own frightened ones, Bron said in explanation, "'Tis the backlash of magic."

He dropped the pitcher and half turned from her. Her own eyes lowered with the realization. They stood together and apart in a bitter epiphany. The sun might have come up and gone down again.

When at last he moved, it was to encircle her shoulders with a light protective arm. "Forgive me, milady."

Eithne buried her face against his chest. She felt broken, beaten, and betrayed . . . betrayed by her own ignorance and by her own dishonesty. She was like a prisoner in a cage where the gate swung open, but still she could not find her way out.

"Come," said Bron. "'Tis time to speak with Sheelin."

Eithne stepped away. *What about?*

"The truth."

Her head shook slowly back and forth with resistance. *Nay, 'twill only be worse on us.*

"Why do you say this?"

I know.

"Eithne," he said in a gentle imperative. "You must tell me the truth. What is happening here? Why does Sheelin wish you to speak?"

Her lips tightened.

He reached out and put his fingers to her lips, and under their soft pressure her lips parted slightly. "I know you can speak aloud. I bet you can sing sweetly as well. What keeps you mute? 'Tis not just the stubbornness of an unruly lass."

Beway, do not press me.

He stroked her shoulder reassuringly, dropping his hand to her waist and pulling her close to him. "If you cannot trust, you cannot love."

I have no wish to love. But even as she spoke, she tingled from the power of feeling he stirred in her.

He drew away and took her hand in his own. "'Tis high time for me to speak to Sheelin. I beg you to attend me." He searched her eyes imploringly. "'Tis my neck on the chopping block. I have no wont to die. You need not love me to champion my cause."

She sighed, struggling with his demand and again her own duality. *I do not well abide my father's presence, but this once I will come with you.*

The atmosphere of the room brightened with this compromise. Early morning sun flooded the chamber and added a magic that only reality could conjure.

Within the hour, Eithne led Bron through the maze of Rath Morna to a circular, turreted outer pavilion, used as a gaol for Sheelin's collection of birds.

She told Bron, *Here Sheelin spends his morning and evening hours.* She held back at the entrance. *I will not enter this place. You must go alone, but I will listen.*

"Why won't you come inside?"

You will see. She turned and lowered herself to sit cross-legged upon the ground.

The smell of rotting flesh hit Bron foremost and he covered his nose when he stepped beneath the portico. The interior was as gray as a winter sea . . . and as grimly foreboding. A menagerie of fowl, caged, tethered, and pinioned, met his aghast regard. Listless swans, long necks curled beneath ragged wings, nested on filthy straw. He'd been in dungeons which proved more hospitable.

A hoarse chuckle rumbled from Sheelin's side where the Fir Darrig tore at the flesh and feathers of a dead pigeon with his needlelike teeth. Bron knew enough of Fir Darrigs that by birth they were of low descent, sired by an evil spirit upon a degenerate Ghillie Dhu. This one was less than three feet high and wore a red roundabout, with red breeches buckled at the knee. A black chimney hat tipped crookedly over his hairy, withered face.

Wearing a black fox fur cloak, Sheelin turned around and peered from his heavy-lidded, deep-set eyes. "Ah! Fir Darrig, we have a guest."

The stench was so overpowering that Bron replied, "You have, but do not let me disturb you. I can await you outside."

"Nay, come and you will have the treat of seeing my peerless aviary." And with an upward wave of his hand, Sheelin's menagerie of inhumanity transformed into an exotic display.

Too recently inebriated on magic, Bron experienced a gut-turning distaste. He needed no more illusion, especially at the expense of helpless creatures. Yet, he dared not offend Sheelin.

For the moment, he endured Sheelin's spectacle, watching him closely. There was an aura about him— an air of craftiness, indifference, and deceit. He did not necessarily look evil . . . but then how did evil look? And in this instance which was more evil, the illusion or the reality?

Bron began circumspectly, "'Tis more than impressive."

A self-satisfied smile curled the corners of Sheelin's mouth. "I'm partial to the swans," he confessed stroking the hill-high arch of one's neck.

The faint suspicion that one of these birds might be Ketha, the swan sister, constricted Bron's heart.

Sheelin sprinkled seed about with the grace of a magnificent benefactor. "What is your reason for coming to see me?" he asked. Then he added with a lifted brow, "Has the Lady Eithne been uncooperative?"

"Nay, she is a winsome companion . . . too much so." Bron gave him an even look.

Sheelin laughed suddenly. "Then what is amiss?"

"Nothing is amiss. I wish to leave Rath Morna and take the Lady Eithne with me."

Surprise flashed across Sheelin's features and was quickly concealed. The Fir Darrig burped, his attention taken from his meal.

"And what think you of this, Eithne?" asked Sheelin, his eyes looking past Bron.

Bron stepped back, and behind him in the portico stood Eithne. Disquiet marked her face. *He'll never agree to it,* came her words as surely as if she had spoken aloud.

"'Tis a pity she cannot speak for herself," Sheelin said, his voice deadly cold. "I must decline your offer . . . on her behalf, of course. The agreement stands. The man who can answer in truth a question Eithne will ask, and will ask a question she can in truth answer, should have her for his bride along with riches untold."

"Aye." Bron's voice held the tone of cool derision. "That is the dilemma. There is too much untold and unspoken at Rath Morna."

Eithne shook her head as if to caution him to keep his opinions to himself.

But he would not let it go just yet. "I would ask why 'tis so expedient the Lady Eithne speaks?"

Magnanimity danced lightly through the occult darkness of Sheelin's eyes. "'Twould bring joy to a father's heart . . . a miracle to Rath Morna."

He lies. I beg you, leave it.

Bron glanced at Eithne and briefly met the urgent appeal in her eyes. For her sake, he would let it rest.

Bron's demeanor shifted. "Then I will do my utmost to bring about this miracle. Indeed, my own life truly depends upon it." He bowed slightly and walked toward Eithne.

He saw pain in her expression. He knew that being who she was she would simply suffer in silence rather than confront her father or escape Rath Morna.

Once outside the pavilion, he breathed the fresh morning air into his lungs and expelled the morass of Sheelin's aviary. In silence and deep thought, he and Eithne walked toward the bailey yard. He turned to her. Her eyes held a cloudy, misty, faraway gaze.

I told you 'twas useless to speak with him. Truth cannot pass his lips.

He stared at her a deepening moment, then said, "You have your own brand of dishonesty, milady."

She bridled, her temper flaring. *I never lie and have done nothing dishonest.*

He reached over and gently touched a hand to her shoulder. "You have other ways of being less than truthful. You tell the truth, but only part of it, only what you wish to tell."

Surprise and hurt flicked over her comely features.

He did not mean to wound her, but only find a foothold in her honesty. For honesty alone would be their salvation.

With a toss of her brilliant copper head, she shrugged his hand off and turned her back upon him. Struggling between his own frustration and compassion, he stood quite still and watched her stalk away.

"Blathers! Sheee . . . is throuble! Sartainly, ye've larnt yer lesson."

The voice Bron easily recognized. Gibbers was at his snooping again. Bron turned and spied his beaming moss streaked face poking up from the nearby sinkhole.

Feeling beaten, Bron walked over and sat down beside Gibbers. "You seem to know so much about women. What would you advise I do to get to the bottom of it?"

He grimaced, a gleeful spark in his eyes. "You'll niver get the truth at Rath Morna."

"And what is the truth?"

"Musha. I'll niver tell."

"Niver?" mocked Bron. "Surely you have a price."

His mouth cracked open like a bottomless cavern. "Indade I have."

"What is it?" Bron tried to be playful, but beneath it he wanted to reach over and squeeze the green-veined cords of Gibbers's scrawny neck.

"Shhhweets. I'm partial to sugar violets."

"Sugar violets." Bron chuckled. "Very well, you shall have your sugar violets. Now speak."

"Begobs, do ye think me a divil's fool to spake a'fore I've me tribute?"

"Mayhap you think me the fool to give you sweets and then learn nothing. Nay, I will ask you one question. If your answer pleases me, then, you'll have your sweets," Bron said equitably, gambling that Gibbers craved his "shhhweets" enough to risk telling beforehand.

Gibbers hissed his vexation.

Bron merely yawned and shrugged. "And to think while I walked in the woods yesterday I passed a patch of violets in full bloom." He glanced sidelong. Gibbers was fairly salivating. The temperament of a troll was mixed; not wholly good nor entirely evil, but balanced between the two, sometimes generous, then descending to petty meanness.

"Ye slatherin' tormentor, ask yer question, but only one. I'll have my shhhweets by sunrise . . . or I'll sarve ye ill."

Bron concealed his delight and his spirits began to elevate. He had a thousand questions, but could only ask one. Which one?

He fingered his chin thoughtfully.

"Begorra, cud ye make haste?"

"Aye, aye . . ." Of all the riddles that traversed his mind, the most obvious came to his lips. "Why will Eithne not speak?"

"Musha, cud ye not ask one harder? A pooka cud tell ye that. Ye've frittered—"

"Enough!" Bron declared, his patience gone. "Tell me the answer if you can or be off."

Gibbers's pointed ears twitched and he leered at Bron. "Humph! The wicked gurrul will not spake fer right reason. She was born with the singer's voice. Sheelin will grab her voice and the seycrets of that power."

It made perfect sense . . . aye, he thought, a pooka could have told me. "Where does Eithne disappear to at night?"

"Lave off yerself! 'Tis only one question I'll answer." With that, Gibbers slipped down into the sinkhole. "A morrow at sunrise ... my shhh-weets ... !" his voice lisped as he disappeared.

Bron was left to ruminate over his predicament. He must decide his priority. Was it to find Ketha or to rescue a resistant Eithne from her father's evil? Mayhap both ... and mayhap one would lead to the other. But first he must win Eithne's trust ... and how was that to be done? Stubbornness and defiance were her second nature. Arrah! that was the question he should have posed to Gibbers. How to win Eithne's trust?

Chapter
9

It was twilight.

The sun had set in a purple burning which spread soft hues over halfheaven. A solitary star rose in the east. Bron gazed above the cashel walls to the rising moon on the deepening blue horizon.

Whistling a lilting tune, he groomed Samisen's snowy coat. The stallion's flanks rippled with pleasure. Over the broad slope of the horse's shoulders, he kept the tower in view. Eithne's silhouette was framed in the window casement. He knew she knew he watched her. She'd been pacing. Now she sat quietly. Had she expected him to come to her chambers this night? Did she pace from disappointment or an overburdened conscience?

"Aye," he said softly in Samisen's ear. "She's restless this night. I wager she'll fly before midnight. Be ready. She'll not tarry for us."

He gave Samisen a handful of grain, then he stretched his length on a grassy patch. The scents of sweetbriar and hyacinth wafted over the cashel walls.

Night birds warbled in the woods beyond the moat. Sighing deeply, he could not feel more relaxed. He clasped his hands behind his head and settled comfortably to wait.

A dunlin's *whilloo* woke Bron from his dozing. His eyes flew to the tower. The window gaped open. Leaping to his feet, he caught Samisen's trailing white mane and climbed upon his back.

He began a rhythmic chanting as ancient as the sea. Samisen pawed the earth with a silver shod hoof. In a final command Bron said softly, "Unfold your wings and take flight."

The stallion reared, snorting and tossing its head, and then plunged upward . . . into the air. Bron held tightly as the great wings miraculously fanned out and lifted them both skyward. The night wind sliced across Bron's face, filling him with expectancy and exhilaration. Up . . . up . . . above cashel wall, above turreted towers and spearing treetops, rider and winged-steed flew.

He searched the shadowy landscape for any trace of Eithne. By and by, Samisen carried him toward the deserted moorlands of the North. The rising moon cast an eerie light over lonely marshes and cattail choked quagmires. With disappointment growing, Bron doubted she would seek out this wild realm. Then he saw it . . . or did he?

He blinked and squinted into the darkness below. A short word to Samisen and the stallion began a lowering spiral. Mayhap he was mistaken, but Bron thought he saw a tower rising up from the marsh.

The horse stooped to find foothold among the reeds

where the mud could barely hold him up. Not far, out in the middle of a large stretch of pond, rose the gnarled old stump of what once had been a great tree . . . or was it? Fingers of mist distorted his vision until he perceived that aye, there was a tower there . . . and then in the next moment it was a tree stump. More illusion?

He urged Samisen onward into the murky water. The stallion shied slightly. "I know you do not wish your fine coat soiled, but put your vanity aside, 'tis a mystery we're about solving."

There was little solid ground, but Bron trusted his steed's instinctual sense to carry them safely along. The closer he came the more substantial became the vision of the tower, until he reached to touch cold stone.

"Aye, 'tis a tower . . . mayhap abandoned. And built for what purpose I cannot guess," he spoke aloud to himself. Guiding Samisen around its base, he soon discovered it had no entrance. The only opening was a tiny casement window high above facing to the south.

"Hallo!" he called out. The wind twisted his voice into a faint howl. He had no expectation anyone would answer. It was too lonely a place.

At that moment Samisen lost his footing and down he stumbled into the scrotum-numbing waters, dousing Bron to the hips.

"Arraah!" he gasped. "Let's be off."

And with that, Samisen reared and plunged upward, gaining lift in a strong pull of wings.

Sometime later, Bron spied the holy circle of stones

outside Rath Morna. He remembered his promise to Gibbers and realized that he must make good his word. Circling, he saw below the small copse of beechwood surrounding the spring fed pond. It would be a good spot to recuperate. Samisen could graze and he could search for violets . . . though in the darkness he might not have great success.

The pair came to rest beside the pond. He dismounted and let Samisen wander. He stripped off his brackish smelling clothing, winged his arms with vigor, and plunged in the tepid pond with a deep-throated shout.

It was the perfect night for a moonlight swim. Too bad he must be alone. Too bad he had slept too long and missed following the elusive Eithne. Floating upon his back like a turtle on a summer pond, he imagined her being there with him. But he was foolish to dream for it would only bring disillusionment in the end. Aye, heartbreak was the price of love's ecstasy.

After a time, he climbed from the water onto the mossy bank. Beside him splashed Samisen, shaking the water from his withers and spraying diamond drops with the toss of his mane.

"Be away with you!" grumbled Bron, slapping the horse's flank with his hand. "Go roll yourself in a bed of blossoms."

He did not bother to dress himself, but like a spriggan, he walked naked into the woods to search for violets.

He had a good nose and it was not long before the

subtle, sweet fragrant scent stole from beneath furze and fern. Indeed, 'twas a fool's task to pluck violets in the dark of night and then he must go to the kitchen and dip them in sugared froth. All this before dawn or he would lose his best tattler.

Crawling about on his knees, he not only felt the fool but the acute disadvantage of his one-handedness. Mayhap he'd be the wiser to wait until dawn. Even so, he persevered through thicket and briar, hawthorn and hedge.

When he returned, a hard won nosegay of violets in hand, Samisen grazed contentedly. What next captured Bron's attention was the silhouette of a lone white swan on the water. Its silk-soft neck arched hill high, it preened and glided serenely on the moon-mirroring surface.

Some things one just knew. And he knew it was his Lady Eithne. He lay the nosegay beside his clothing and stepped back into the water. Eddying swirls lapped his body, exciting him as surely as a touch.

As he moved closer the swan glided farther away, leaving ripples in its wake.

"Arrah! I've no heart for magic this night. Show yourself to me, my Lady Eithne," he challenged outright.

The swan continued to skirt the outer perimeters of the pond. He knew a true wild creature would not court him, but would have flown when he first appeared. Almost immediately he realized aggressiveness would get him nowhere. He tried a new tack, turned over, and floated in place. Gazing at the starry heavens above, he whistled indifferently. On occasion, in a sidelong glance, he caught the movement of the swan circling closer to him.

Finally, he stopped whistling. Silence, still as an hourglass, reigned. The swan drifted nearer.

"Don't fear it," he said softly, and wondered if he spoke to her or himself. It was no easy thing to open oneself to true love. In that moment, under night's secret shade, he sensed he might make claim to true loving.

Cunningly, the swan disappeared beneath the obsidian water and a few seconds later surfaced, a full-fleshed woman . . . glistening droplets of water falling from her hair.

He gazed into her eyes . . . and like his dream, he saw the pouring forth of pure love.

In trembling voice, his mind anxious, he softly whispered, "I love you, Lady Eithne."

She blushed and smiled so warmly that his fears fell away.

He was not sure who moved to whom first, but her arms were suddenly around his neck and his hands were on her smooth hips. Her yielding form he pressed close, and with a deep-felt sigh he surrendered to desire. He was pulling her in slow circles through the water. They stared into each other's eyes soulfully. Hers glistened with the pale fire of stars.

Beway, sea clansman. I am afraid.

"No more than I am myself. After this night there will be few secrets between us."

Why did you not tell me you've a flying steed?

"Mayhap the same reason you did not tell me you

were a flying swan. What other secrets do you with-hold from me?"

Her body nudged against his, inflaming him. He swallowed hard. She was indeed beautiful and irresist-ible.

As many as I choose . . . And who are you that you ride a steed of the Tuatha de Danann? Surely you have more secrets, Bron mac Llyr.

Her features held a hint of wary trust. He knew that he must abide her way of cautiously manifesting herself in layers. It was the movement of her pupils and the curl of her lips, a fear of being outmaneu-vered. He must be patient, but not too patient. His awareness of her thighs and breasts brushing against him was so acute, it was almost pain.

"'Tis no secret that I am the son of the sorcerer sea king Manannan mac Llyr."

Her eyes widened. *I did not know this. Does my father?*

"Nay, he knows only that I search for the healer Ketha."

Ketha!

He felt her surprise. "Aye, Ketha. She is the one woman in Banba that might restore my hand."

Her black-winged brows arched with surprise. *Why did you not tell me this before?*

"I did, the first night of my arrival . . . in your father's hall."

I did not hear it . . . then I came late.

Not taking his eyes from her he said with underly-ing intensity, "Do you know of Ketha? You must tell me."

Her dark lashes lowered. *Ketha is my mother.*

"You are a swan witch as well?"

Aye.

"Can you take me to her?"

Her features became troubled. *Nay, I do not know where she is. My father imprisoned her many years ago. I fly at night searching. Sometimes I fear . . . she is no more.* Tears slipped down her cheeks.

With compassion, Bron leaned to her and kissed the welling over of her despair. The taste was salty upon his lips, reminding him of his sea home. He remembered the loss of his own mother, who sailed away to the faraway isles when he was very young.

"Beway . . . beway . . ." he comforted softly. Her delicate breast rose and fell with long repressed emotion. He slipped an arm under her knees, lifting her from the water. On the bank he set her upon her feet and together, hands clasping, they walked to the circle of stones. As if invisibly led, they came upon a fairy ring of white mushrooms in the circle's center. He gazed at her and she at him in a harmonious knowing. It was love's magic.

Eithne sat down beneath a moon that poured out light like a shower of pearls, and drew him to her. He looped his arm and she leaned into him. "I have naught to cover you with, but my own nakedness."

Her bare skin shone pearlescent. The water beaded like tiny crystals over her small, firm breasts and belly. In an act of modesty, she pulled her slim legs up in front of her and coiled her arms around her knees.

'Tis all right. We are exposed before each other now, you have seen my swanself.

"Why did you not reveal this to me before?"

I could not. I feared you were in league with my father. Once he has the power of my voice he intends to invade Myr and rule there with his Unseelie Court. His scheme to break me is more successful than he could have imagined. Though Bron had already learned much from Gibbers, he was stunned by the extent of Sheelin's ambition. Eithne sighed. *I ache to speak . . . yearn to sing . . . and now that you have come something else has happened to me.*

"What?"

She did not send her thoughts to him. She looked into his eyes, filling him and emptying him in a glance. As surely as if she'd spoken aloud he knew what had happened to her, for it had happened to him as well.

His heart was beating a bludgeoning pace and he felt arousal mounting in his body. The power of his desire burned and flamed into his limbs. Yet, his disfigurement kept him constrained. His sense of manliness and his fear of vulnerability caused him to hesitate . . . thinking he'd best stand and clothe himself.

He made to draw back, but the promise in her marsh-fire eyes held him in place.

Love me, came her silent plea.

"Arraah," he sighed hoarsely. He felt like a drowning man, and his senses lashed and thundered like waves on a treacherous coast.

Imploringly, her hands splayed across his bare chest. He felt the tips of her nails graze his skin.

Though I cannot speak it aloud, I call you to my arms . . . to my heart.

Like a butterfly, her lips alighted to kiss the base of his throat. Her breasts and long silken hair brushed his chest and he felt his own nipples harden in anticipation.

This was not illusion. She wanted him. There would be no shape-shifting, no magic or sleeping potions this night.

The taste, touch, and feel of her was real . . . soaringly so.

Eithne drew back. She lifted her eyes to Bron's and saw reflected in them her own inner fears and doubts. She had no wish to bewitch him or dazzle him with magic. On this night, under this moon, she sought "true loving."

Everything about him aroused her desire. The shadowy depths of his sea-watching eyes that were sometimes mocking and sharp; his confident benevolent disposition that bespoke gentleness and generosity . . . the funny way he whistled. Her perusal strayed to his flat wine-dark male nipples, over his broad chest smooth with male muscle, down the full length of his sinuous torso where the spear of his manhood swelled. He was strong, so vibrant in his maleness, so sure. All this and more captured her heart.

Love me true, she pleaded in an unspoken request.

"I do and will." He sighed, completely disarmed. "You need not ask." His hands cupped her face gently, and he held her gaze. "I'll love you true . . . my swan witch."

She touched his face, and his mouth lowered to

hers. She melted against his warm bare skin, sliding her hands over his chest and twining her fingers around his neck. She closed her eyes, swimming into the liquid pleasures of their kiss. A kiss without enchantment, but wholly enchanted.

He kissed her lushly and long, with a caressing intensity that left her limp everywhere. She embraced him wholeheartedly, sinking into the essence of his virility. She felt his hands travel slowly, exploring the curves of her hips and waist. He lowered his head and kissed the white curve of her shoulder. With his tongue, he traced lower, to the swell of her breasts. His mouth swooped lower and caught a piquant nipple between his lips and gently suckled her.

Her breath stopped. Sweet, sweet goddess! Goose bumps shimmered over her skin. Her hands caressed his lowered head, and her lips kissed the black sheen of his unbound hair splaying across his muscled back.

Softly stretching, she lay upon the mossy turf. He moved his long length beside her, cushioning her in his strong arms. Her eyes searched the moon-fired depths of his own. His gaze set fires in her belly and beneath her ribs. Her breast throbbed and she felt her spirit rush outward to encompass his.

"You are beautiful, swan witch," his deep voice purred. "When I first saw you leaning over the parapet, I thought you were a witch. Now I know I was not far wrong."

And I thought you a fool. Beway . . . I thank the fates for fools, she revealed, wondering if she might die of delight.

A chuckle vibrated his chest while an inflaming gaze lit his eyes. He lowered his mouth to hers. Lightly, he nuckered the moist, soft sides of her lower and upper lips. Her mouth relaxed. She felt his tongue slip into her mouth, past pearl teeth. Slowly, he ran its tip across the roof of her mouth and licked the satiny folds of her inner cheek.

An exquisite ticklish sensation rippled through her as a subtle wetness suddenly watered her mouth like dewy honey. Long crushed desire exploded in her. She released a slow breath of surrender and boldly laved the slick heat of his cunning tongue.

While kissing her, he bestowed continuous caresses with the palm of his hand over her shoulders, following the swell of her breasts down the soft flesh of her belly. With the lightest brushing of his fingertips, he circled the soft indentation of her stomach, moving down to the secret nest of her womanhood. He aroused her in ways she'd never imagined in dreaming moments, and never thought to experience. Aye, 'twas better than magic!

He pressed gently with the heel of his hand on her woman's mound. Fire shot through her. She arched to the pressure of his palm and yawned to the full swell of his tongue. He withdrew from her and kissed the hollow of her throat.

In a hoarse, passion-skirted whisper, he said, "Fly with me this night on wild wings of love. . . ."

The poetry of his words filled Eithne, but she could speak none of her own aloud. His words had touched her, and in the mystical way of her kith she longed to sing her love lilt . . . a swan song, a ritual of disclosure and bonding.

He buried his lips in the furrow of her cleavage and kissed the pulse of her heart. Little by little she felt his tongue preen the full circle of her breast. He nuzzled and lapped, secreting his tongue's tip along the half-moon fold beneath.

Soon his head dipped down to rain hot kisses upon the hollow of her belly, and her desire spread like fever to tingle every nerve. His kisses were long and deeply sensuous as if he sucked into himself her very essence.

His hands slipped around and cupped the pillow of her hips. His dark head lowered, and his mouth gently met the inner velvet of her thighs. She relished the moist stroking creeping up inside each leg in turn. His tongue moved in soft swirls along the outer boundaries of her woman's mound. Unhurried, as if he intended to sup on every cream-flushed pore, he tasted the moist folds of her sensitive confines. She felt soft contractions and realized her virginal channel expanded, readying to embrace his shaft. She ached, feeling the soft surge again, and again.

She reached for him, clasping his thick hair in her fists, and drew his face up to her own. In the starlight she could see the flash of his teeth as he smiled.

I'm dying for you, she begged with the full potency of her emotion.

His arms encircled her.

Her body twisted, reaching to the heat of his engorged manhood. She felt his chest rise and fall in rhythmic coursing against her own. Again he put his mouth on hers, sucking tenderly on her upper lip, using his tongue and lips to imbibe the moist, pulpy underflesh. A wild heat fired her blood and she became bold and kissed him as he kissed her—meeting his tongue, moving her lips against his.

Instinctively, she spread her legs, arching up to him. He met her wantonness with his own urgency. Her hands clung to the lean hardness of his hips, guiding him to her. Gathering himself, he entered slowly . . . straining against her silken, virginal cloak of last resistance.

"Sweet witch!" he groaned, full-throated, as he thrust deep his shaft into the dark body of her womb. She felt the fingers of his one hand roughly clutch her shoulder.

"Arra-a-ah!" he shouted aloud, like a warrior's battle cry.

Eithne saw his pain flash like wildfire in the contracting spokes of his pupils. She felt a tremendous pang of guilt. Mayhap she should have warned him it would be painful . . . but only briefly so. But if she had warned him, he might not have loved her. Oh . . . too many secrets.

'Tis but fleeting. I do not betray you. Your ecstasy will come . . . a hundredfold. Hold back, my sea clansman. I will promise you a mating like no other you have known.

In his eyes she witnessed his struggle for mastery. Moisture beaded the shadow of his mouth, she kissed it away. Between the brokenness of breath, the primordial panic, she felt the rippling epiphany of love unfold.

On slow wing, their spirit dance began.

His strokes became more powerful. Together, their hips undulating, the one potent, the other yielding. Simultaneously strong and soft, thrusting and withdrawing. No space was between them . . . a single body, a single breath, a single pulsating. Bliss rushed with delicious force from her womb, setting a long fire in her belly, onto her breast, catapulting like shooting stars across hot heaven.

Whirlwinds of delight carried Eithne sky-high. . . .

Their union was like a dawning daylight rainbow carrying them upward into deep wonder . . . downward into silent pools of crystalline communion.

At last, her heart unbound, she was free to love with nothing withheld. She was no longer the wicked, evil "gurrul" . . . but a wild-winged shapeshifter soaring to ecstasy.

The air rustled with the wind of wing, she transformed into swan . . . down and feathers wafted in the air . . . she floated on the currents of sun-spilled eternity . . . and then just as quickly she reshaped into woman.

She felt his heart pounding next to her own, and she held him close with joy and awe. In the eddying waves of rapture, she drew a trembling breath and opened her tear-moistened eyes to seek his own. In that connecting, she glimpsed his mystery, his depths and shallows . . . the falling away of every mask.

Her soul bursting, she met his emerald gaze. *I love you. I have always loved you.*

"You love because you are loved. You have enchanted me without enchantment, my swan witch."

'Tis only the beginning . . .

Again, his mouth was upon hers and his kisses rushed upon her like the wild waves of the sea.

Chapter
10

"The top o' the day to ye, sweethearts," gargled the provoking voice of Gibbers. "Begorrah, whare've ye been? I'm waitin' since sunup fer me tribute."

Startled to wakefulness, Eithne sat up, beside her Bron stirred as well. Through the night he'd pleasured her until she felt as joyously radiant as the sun above.

Sun? Beway! She squinted eastward to the golden orb rising full face above the stone circle. Disbelieving the hours had passed so quickly, she felt uneasy.

Be off! glared Eithne, attempting to gather her wits. Gibbers lurched forward a step.

"Niver! I'll throuble ye to keep yer word, Bron mac Llyr." His gob green orbs widened and he pointed a spidery finger. "Look a ye, gurrul. Ye aren't dacent."

"Leave off!" Bron said sharply. "I'll be good to my word."

"Too late!" cackled Gibbers with so much maliciousness that Bron rose to his feet threateningly.

Gibbers scrambled off and hid behind a dolmen.

"Come," said Bron to Eithne. Gently kissing her

cheek, he looped his arm protectively around her shoulders and led her to where he had left his clothing. He gave her his cloak and slipped on his own tunic, leggings, and boots.

He caught the reins of Samisen's bridle. He hefted the saddle onto the horse's back, then retied his harp and kit bag to the saddle leathers. "What do you wish to do?"

Her breast rose and fell in a deep sigh. She was not sure. She reached up and touched the stubble of whiskers on his cheeks. Light speared the glowing filament of his irises. Though his features appeared relaxed there was a steely gravity in his eyes.

What did she wish to do? In the aftermath of his loving everything had changed. She trusted him. She trusted him because she trusted herself with him. How that alchemy had transpired she was not sure. Had it happened when at last she'd told the truth of it all to him? Or did it begin from the first instance she saw him cross the bridge of buzzards?

I wish to go with you, Bron mac Llyr. I wish to go to the isles of the sea . . . to your home on stone cliffs. All this I wish. But these are only wishes. I dream . . . my dreams are like the illusions of Rath Morna.

"You doubt your dreams?"

Beway . . . dreams are for those who sleep.

"Mayhap your doubts hold the illusions in place. You could be free, my swan heart. Free."

And how can I be free?

He pulled her close. Her arms wrapped around him in a fragile embrace, and she rested her cheek against the strength of his chest. "I have told you in words and deed. . . . You must love more than you fear."

I do not know how not to fear! Tears slipped down her cheeks and she raised her hand to brush them away. *I have always feared.*

She felt Bron's warmth and love, but she still feared.

"Oho . . . ohoo! They be here!" came Gibbers's alarming cry. He ran from behind a great stone into the circle center.

Eithne pulled away from Bron and riveted her gaze beyond the stones. She saw her father and his Unseelie Court approaching across the bridge. Her mouth dropped open as if she were going to cry out herself. Aye, she trembled with the fear of him.

Panic striking her, she tore herself from Bron's arms. She ran toward Gibbers and in a mighty effort caught hold of his jumping body and ruthlessly shook him.

You've betrayed us . . . you little demon! You've betrayed us!

"Ye betrayed yerselves," he screeched, bursting with that horrid laugh he had. "I know all yer sssecrets . . . and quare things. I know whare ye go at night . . . I know whare yer mother's imprisoned. . . I know—"

My mother? Her hands gripped his throat. *Where is she? Where!* Aye, he'd known all these years and withheld it from her. The very devil he was! 'Twas the end of his tormenting, the last of his insults and taunting.

His bulging eyes bulged more . . . his green face began turning green-blue. Overwrought and unable to express aloud her outrage, Eithne's breast heaved from the containment of it and she squeezed his neck harder and harder.

Bron came up behind her and he caught her wrist in his hand. "Eithne, Eithne . . . you must stop. 'Twill do no good to choke him . . . though well he deserves it."

She released him abruptly. Gibbers gimped into a fetal ball and groaned. She covered her face with her hands in all-out weeping.

"Beway . . . dearest one." Bron gathered her in the comforting blanket of his arms.

Gibbers gasped for breath. "Ye murdherin' gurrul!"

"What goes on?" rang Sheelin's voice from outside the stone circle.

"Naught that involves you, Sheelin," returned Bron.

"As you like." Then, "However, I am here on my own errand."

"He kin't enter the circle of stones . . ." whispered Gibbers.

Bron looked down at him curiously. "Not more secrets?"

Gibbers's one eye narrowed with canniness and he smirked, "Aye, more secrets . . . none of thim kin."

"Why?"

"I'll niver tell!" He threw back his head with a delightful croak.

Eithne all but reached out to grab his neck again, but Bron's arms stopped her.

Bron muttered an oath under his breath. The wretch knew no bounds or how close he truly came to being murdered.

"Is something amiss?" called Sheelin, his demeanor gratuitous.

Gathering herself, Eithne ceased her weeping. She stared at her father and his Unseelie Court, bedecked in the false finery of lords and ladies, looming just beyond the stones. Above their heads fluttered banners of bright colors and they mingled with a festive air as if a tournament or . . . beheading was to ensue.

Bron left Eithne and walked toward Sheelin. As far as he was concerned the charade was finished—too many secrets, too much illusion.

Cloaked in black, Sheelin stood like a holy man, his hands clasped self-righteously over his heart. Rabidly, the Fir Darrig was running on all fours around the henge—to and fro like a wild hyena awaiting the kill.

"Aye, Sheelin. All is amiss." Bron stepped outside the circle and walked toward Sheelin. He did not see the blow that knocked him to his knees, but he did see Coup de Grace, axe in hand, standing beside a stump of a chopping block so conveniently hidden behind Sheelin. He still counted Coup friend and knew he was not responsible for the debilitating blow. Two of Sheelin's gillies held him motionless, while another tied his hands behind him.

"I think not," declared Sheelin, indifferent as stone. "I've made the decision to hasten your ordeal. I am a compassionate man and I do not abide suffering very well."

In the periphery of his vision Bron saw Eithne running across the circle. Instinctively, he knew she must not leave its boundaries. "Stay where you are," he commanded.

She halted.

"Have you any last requests?" Sheelin's deep black eyes slipped away from Eithne and then querulously to Bron.

"Aye, there is one thing," announced Bron. "I would like my hair pulled forward away from my neck so it won't be soiled with my blood."

It was no surprise to him when the Fir Darrig sprang forward and seized hold of his hair. He twisted it punishingly tight around his clawlike hands.

Sheelin turned to his daughter. "'Tis time Eithne to ask your question . . . and save your hero." His tone was spiced with lashing sarcasm.

Bron looked over to Eithne. He'd hoped it would not come to this. She stood precariously close to the outer boundary of the henge. Her face was drained of color and her crimson hair flamed wild in the sun. She seemed a tormented specter. Her gaze fastened onto Bron like a drowning soul in a storm ravaged sea.

His life hung in balance with the fate of Myr. He would not sway her and composed his features with blandness. How would he himself choose?

The words struggled out with shocking clarity across her long silent lips. "Do you love me, Bron mac Llyr?"

For the space of a heartbeat he hesitated. Her voice was rich and resonant and oddly familiar. "Aye, Eithne. I love you. And do you love me?"

"With all my heart." He saw her love in her eyes and he did not doubt.

"Coup!" snapped Sheelin, dispassionately. "Sever his head!"

Bron heard Coup's questioning challenge. "Mi-lord?"

The Fir Darrig viciously yanked Bron's head forward.

"Now!" reaffirmed Sheelin, without a care to fair play.

Bron heard Eithne's scream . . . a fierce denial. A cry that ripped asunder mind and heart . . . a cry that echoed through the forest and reverberated through the deserted towers of Rath Morna.

"Be wise, friend," counseled Coup under his breath, and he lifted his axe.

Bron jerked back . . . pulling the Fir Darrig forward.

The axe fell . . . slicing off the Fir Darrig's hands. Black blood sprayed everywhere.

Then Bron felt the bond being severed at his wrists. "Run for yer freedom," cried Coup.

Bron needed no prodding. He leaped to his feet and ran into the confines of the stone circle. He whistled to Samisen. Snorting and head shaking, the horse galloped toward him. Bron swept Eithne up into his arms and onto the horse.

Jumping on himself, he paused for a split second. Gibbers! He leaned dangerously forward, nearly unbalancing himself and caught the little devil by the neck.

"Begobs . . . let me be! I'm afeerin' heights. Nay! nay!" he squealed.

Bron ignored his protests and gave the command to his horse to fly. Samisen reared on hind legs, pawing the air, and lunged upward. His powerful wings spread and lifted the riders high above the stone circle, high above the turrets of Rath Morna and beyond the grasp of Sheelin.

Bron continued to hold Gibbers outstretched. Gibbers cried and flailed his scrawny arms pathetically, grabbing for the safety of the stallion's back. "Tell us now where Ketha is imprisoned or I'll be dropping you."

"I'll niver tell!" bawled Gibbers.

"My fingers grow weary . . . and mark I have but one hand. Once I let go . . . I let go," threatened Bron.

"I'll have me tribute . . ." whined Gibbers, his own fingers clawing the empty air for a handhold.

"Speak, you bog child," rasped Eithne. "Speak or I'll shout your own secrets o'er the countryside."

She was clasping her throat as if it pained her to speak.

"What is it?" asked Bron, worriedly.

"'Tis . . . 'tis Sheelin. He draws off my voice."

"Is there no way to stop him?"

"My mother . . . we must find my mother."

Bron turned his attention to Gibbers. "Speak now, you green imp! Or I'll dust the mountain peaks with your carcass."

"Troth! I dunno . . . only 'tis in the northern marssshes . . ."

"The northern marshes. Arrah!" Bron knew the place. He tossed Gibbers into Eithne's arms and muttered a cryptic word in Samisen's ear.

"You know?" asked Eithne, half-heartedly patting Gibbers, who shivered with fear in her arms like a fresh cream pudding.

"I know. The night past, while searching for you I found a tower in the marshes. I believed it to be deserted. It had no entrance, only a single lancet window high above."

"I have never spied a tower in the northern marshes. I have flown over it a hundred times."

"'Tis invisible. Another of Sheelin's illusions."

"Nay . . ." breathed Eithne, peering over the wide wings of Samisen.

Around them the gathering storm clouds veiled the sun and the sky paled. Eithne felt chilled and found little comfort from the nearness of the cold-blooded Gibbers. Yet at her back, the warmth of Bron radiated against her skin like a hearth fire.

As they neared the marshlands the skies turned darker and a great wind brewed. Bron guided the horse downward. The tower would be difficult to find again in the vast loneliness that stretched out before them. Fingers of fog clouded vision, but Bron kept his eyes open for the ancient tree stump.

"Will Sheelin follow?" asked Bron.

"Aye, he will follow to hell's door and beyond." Eithne frowned at Gibbers, who hid his face in the folds of her tunic. "Why can't Sheelin and his court enter the circle of stones, Gibbers? And do not say you'll 'niver' tell or I'll throw you off this beastie myself."

He peeked up at her. "A-a-a-h, woorroo, ye should know. 'Tis a lay path into Myr . . . to yer mother's swan clan. Only the pure of heart kin enter."

"Begorrah!" exclaimed Eithne. "Aye, it makes sense now. When I was a child my mother said as much when we walked past the stones. She said, 'There is another world. It is hidden in this one.' I never understood."

"Arrah!" shouted Bron. "I see the tower! Just beyond, through the mists . . . there . . ."

Eithne spied the tower, its outline oscillating in the air, a stone phantasm. Samisen spiraled around its pinnacle.

In the broken lulls between the gusts of wind, Bron cried out, "Lady, help!"

And within the shadows of the casement, Eithne glimpsed the unforgettable fire of her mother's hair . . . a fire that matched her own locks. "Mother!" she cried out.

A slim hand reached between the iron bars. "Eithne? . . . 'Tis you?"

"Aye, we've come . . . but Sheelin is not long behind. My voice . . . he draws away my voice." The cold wind burned her eyes and tears streamed down her reddened cheeks. "You must tell me what to do."

"Sing! Sing to break his illusion . . . as you did when you were a child. The tower cannot withstand the singer's voice."

In the moment Eithne gathered herself. It had been so long since she'd sung. Her throat ached, her whole body ached from resisting the grasping potency of Sheelin's powers.

Her song carried over the desolate marsh, past the soft blue ooze above the bending reeds and out to sea. She sang steadily, her voice growing firm and strong. Against the white fury of the worsening winds, breast heaving, she sang as if winging on the brink of heaven and hell. Deep from her long silenced soul, her full-throated song began splitting foundations and shattering the careful stonework of Sheelin's illusion.

Slowly, the casement cracked wide and fearlessly Ketha lunged forward. The strong arms of Bron caught her to the safety of Samisen's back. Ketha threw her arms around her daughter in a sweet reunion.

Being crushed between the pair Gibbers squealed with irritation, but was readily silenced by Bron. "If it's a might too close for you, we can remedy it quick enough."

In fear of being thrown off, Gibbers squealed again and gripped Ketha's feathered cloak for dear life.

Bron guided Samisen away from the collapsing tower to a solid grassy islet in the marsh. All dismounted. Gibbers fairly kissed the earth, vowing he'd not climb onto that beastie again.

Hands on Eithne's shoulders, Ketha was admiring her. "You've turned into a beauty."

Eithne smiled at her mother, her heart rejoicing. "'Tis your own gift to me."

"And who is this?" asked Ketha, turning to Bron mac Llyr.

A sparkle in her eye, Eithne laid her hand on Bron's arm and said, "He is Bron mac Llyr, the one suitor who could answer the one question that I in truth could ask."

"Nay," breathed Ketha in an admiring tone. "You must tell me all. What was this question?"

A blush suffused Eithne's cheeks. "I asked him if he loved me."

"Bedad," muttered Gibbers, rolling his great round eyes.

"And?" prompted Ketha, giving Gibbers a scolding glance.

"And I said in truth I did," Bron said, taking Eithne's hand and squeezing affectionately.

"Well," declared Ketha, "I will hear the whole story, but first we must make plans as to what we should do now. Without doubt Sheelin is about his own plottings."

"Aye," agreed Eithne, her hand lifted to clutch her aching throat.

At that moment everyone's attention shifted. Across the sky appeared, snowy and huge, five swans winging on the wind toward them. The swans circled above twice, thrice, coming lower each time and then with a flapping of wings skidded along the marsh surface, their legs breaking water into a series of silvery arcs. Alighting silently, their wings closed.

Eithne opened her mind to them.

Sisters, we are couriers from Myr. We've been sent by Bree, the seeress. She summons you to return.

Very well, returned Ketha wordlessly. *I will do what Bree has asked. But you must swear in turn to do what I shall ask of you.*

By our lives, we swear it, sister.

This is my daughter, Eithne, the only woman-child of my line. She is in great danger, yet she cannot return to Myr for in doing so will endanger our land. I will return to Myr, but I ask that three of you, my sisters, remain guardian at my daughter's side wherever she travels.

Eithne did not like this. She turned to her mother and said, "Mother, we have just been reunited. Why must we part? I do not understand?"

"The power of the singer's voice is the only power that can keep Sheelin from breaching the portal between the two worlds of Myr and man. You must remain in the world of men and hold him at bay."

"But even now he draws from me my voice. I cannot keep him from taking what he wants."

"You can, Eithne . . . and you must. Do not underestimate your own power . . . that ancient and rare gift of the singer's voice." She embraced Eithne, holding her a long while as if she were transferring some of her own slender strength to her.

Tears clouded Eithne's eyes and she confessed, "I'm afraid, Mother."

"I know . . . I know," said Ketha, stroking her head. "But you will be in good hands. Go with this man who loves you. His love will be a protection to you." To Bron she said, "Take care of her, Bron mac Llyr." She turned back to the swans. *I will go with you now.*

Ketha stepped off the bank, magically transforming before all eyes into a swan. She and the other two swans, wings flapping, rose heavily and flew off toward the horizon. The other three swans uttered a sonorous farewell and remained floating within sight in the rushes.

Eithne watched the birds disappear.

It became very still.

Bron was eager to leave the marshes and be off to the sea isles of his home, but he was hesitant to press Eithne onward. So much had transpired in the last hours, he thought it best for her to have time to rest. He walked a short distance away and sat down on the bright moss where a green spider laid a gossamer web from reed to reed. Close by, a golden plover arose and flew a little way, its cry stirred the air.

"I'll be havin' ye return me home now," came Gibbers's voice.

Bron near laughed aloud. "I'm not going that way."

Gibbers's mouth dropped wide open, "Och, be aff wid yer nonsinse."

"You won't be returning unless you walk yourself there. The Lady Eithne's safety is foremost. I'll not endanger her by returning to Rath Morna."

Gibbers frowned fiercely. He jabbered his piece of protest about how he'd "niver" find another bridge like the bridge of buzzards or a cashel as much to his liking as Rath Morna.

Bron ignored him and turned his attention to Eithne. She remained still and pensive.

"Wimmin, there's no undhershtandin' thim," philosophized Gibbers, looking at Eithne and shaking his head. "There's rivers that's quiet on top bekase they're deep, an more that's quiet bekase they're not deep enough to make a ripple. An' whin a woman's quiet, begorra, it's not aisy to say if she's deep or shallow."

Bron was not inclined to sit much longer and listen to Gibbers's prattle. "We are leaving now," he announced, coming to his feet. Gibbers scrambled after him, mouthing protests.

Eithne turned when Bron touched her shoulder. "Are you all right?" he asked gently.

She clasped her hand over his and said, "'Tis a lonely place here. I was thinking how it must have been all those years for my mother. How could Sheelin do such a thing to her?"

"It's hard to know why some men do what they do. Come, now. Your mother is free. 'Tis over."

"But not finished." Eithne sighed. She shivered as if icy fingers touched the base of her spine.

The sconces burned low, throwing the chamber in shadow. Sheelin's brow furrowed as he stared into the crystal orb of sight. Through the mists and drifting fragments he saw the ruins of Woad Bog Tower. His face took a stiff, masklike appearance, and grew pale. Ketha had escaped!

The mists of vision shifted to another aspect of the marsh. He saw Bron mac Llyr lifting the blue-cloaked Eithne upon the white stallion. Mac Llyr leaped on himself and the winged steed threw himself upward. Its wings snapped out to seize the wind and it shot away, trailed by three white swans.

Sheelin's thin lips peeled back and he began uttering a low guttural chant while continuing to stare into the crystal orb. The dark bulk of an island suddenly appeared in the mists, rising from the sea like an emerald gem. The last rays of the setting sun burned across its face, touching the small rounded hillocks with shadow and gilding its rocky cliffs golden. On a headland, he saw a circle of great stones. This caused him to fall silent.

With a wave of his hand, the image faded. His eyes hard and sharp, Sheelin turned away.

Chapter

11

'Tis there, Tir nan Og, the Island of Heart's Desire," said Bron. With effort, Eithne opened her eyes. She looked over Samisen's wings and saw tier upon tier of stone mountain rise from the sea. Everything was a deep slate blue and streaked by gray slices of cloud and water. The air was wet and cold and whitecaps frosted the sea.

On the outset it did not appear to her to be a land her heart might desire. And as weary as she felt, it seemed a bleak haven.

"My clan holds a thousand islands in this western sea. They are the Blessed Isles. Some have aught but sheep and gulls, sandy coves and sheltering caves, but 'tis ours to birth and die upon." His voice held pride and the warmth of homecoming.

Daringly, Samisen swooped dangerously near to the stone pinnacles of the sea cliffs. Eithne did not feel well. The journey had been long and arduous. She shifted stiff legs, eager to soon touch her feet to this new land, but apprehensive as well. She worried that she might be unacceptable to his clansmen . . . she who was not of the same kith.

She felt other fears . . . a fear that even surpassed her fear of her father's retribution. She feared that in the end Bron mac Llyr would cast her aside for a woman of his own clan. Now his arms encircled her in protection and love, but would it always be so? Doubt niggled at the corners of her mind. A small wretched voice whispered, *No one can truly love you. You are the evil, wicked gurrul.*

Bron's voice was at her ear, his breath a caress in the chill. "I know a croft where a warm, quiet peat fire burns slowly night and day, where the bed is springy with heather tips and spread with clean white blankets and sleeping furs. A kettle of springwater hangs over the fire, always ready and hot. 'Tis near the white sand beaches where you can walk with me and feel the wind's breath upon your rosy cheeks. There I will take you." Saying this he kissed her.

"Och, and what of me?" moaned Gibbers from his hidey-hole beneath the folds of Eithne's blue cloak.

"I'm thinking there are a myriad of bogs for the likes of you. Take your pick," offered Bron, his head tipping to the vast expanse below, inhabited only by a clump or two of white and black sheep.

"Begorrah, I'll not be nabers with ye swoonin' lovers. The sight fairly turns me stomach."

"Then be off with you!"

And with that, Bron yanked Gibbers from under Eithne's cloak and tossed him from Samisen. Gibbers howled a great walloo. And in the moment even Eithne questioned the intent of Bron's action. But she looked down and saw they were not so far above the marsh bogs. She heard the plop and splash of Gibbers landing in his new abode.

"He'll be fine. 'Tis near enough the croft, but not too near. I should have left him in the northern marsh. He wounds you with his words. I do not like his meanness."

"Aye, he is that, but he was the only playmate of my childhood. I had no others. I would miss him had you left him behind."

"You are too forgiving, Eithne."

"Not so. I near choked him to death."

"Arrah, he earned your ire."

Samisen spiraled lower. Suddenly, Eithne felt him hit solid earth, breaking into a gallop over the rough blanket of turf. Folding in his wings, he soon slowed. The three swans alighted as well upon a small spring fed pond.

In the fading light of evening Eithne saw a rough stone croft tucked against the gray-green scape of moss and lichen covered rockery. Smoke curled from the wind-eye of the slate roof.

A gaggle of brown geese skirting the door yard honked and wing flapped as if to say, who is this come to disturb us? An old sheepdog rose from the doorstep and waggled his tail in greeting.

Bron leaped from Samisen and easily lifted Eithne into his arms. Carrying her, he ducked beneath the overhang and pushed open the latchless door.

Inside, a glowing fish oil lamp on a lace clothed tabletop lightened the natural dimness of the croft. Looking around, Eithne saw it was as Bron had said. A warm fire did burn in the hearth. A bed built into the wooden wall that partitioned off the stable from the croft appeared clean and inviting. A steaming kettle whistled over the fire and beside that butter golden scones sizzled in a pan. Eithne's mouth began to water for it had been some time since she'd eaten.

"Who lives here?" she asked, as he carried her over to the bed and set her down.

"No one," he said, helping her with her feathered cape. He opened a wooden chest at the foot of the bed and took out a down spun shift. "Here, put this on. 'Tis soft and warm."

"But who does it belong to? I cannot wear that which is not mine."

"It belongs to no one and everyone."

Eithne was truly puzzled. "I do not understand."

Bron smiled and said as he walked over to the hearth, "'Tis the way of our clan . . . what belongs to one of us belongs to all of us. Over the islands, here and there, are crofts like this for the wayfarer. In these crofts a fire always burns and food is ever ready." He snatched up a scone and began eating with great relish.

"'Tis magic then."

"Aye, but not of your father's kind. 'Tis the magic of goodness. As long as none succumb to greed our clan ever has abundance. We do not hoard or secret away our bounty. We are openhanded and openhearted."

Eithne had stripped off Bron's tunic and now lifted the down shift over her head. The instant it touched her skin she felt a vibrancy of warmth. The chill departed from her bones and her fingers and toes began to tingle.

"Where is the cashel of your clan?"

"There is naught," he said, still munching.

"Where do they live?"

"Here and there."

"I do not understand."

"My clansmen are loners by habit because of the distances between the islands and solitariness of a seaman's life. Spring, summer, and fall we come together in celebration. Unlike the excess of Rath Morna 'tis a humble feasting. In the winter the seas are unsettled and so we do not gather."

He poured a cup of tea for himself and one for her. He gave it to her. Holding the cup in both her hands, she drank. Her nose began to run from the heat.

"Is there a handkerchief?" she asked.

"Aye." He went to a shelf and reached for a neatly folded handkerchief. She watched him attempt to pick it up with his sword hand. She heard him utter a small curse from under his breath when his fingers passed through it.

She thought a moment and then spoke. "Why do you keep the illusion? We are no longer at Rath Morna," she observed.

In his good hand he gripped the hanky. With his back to her, he stood quite still. There was a barely visible tension across his shoulders as though there were something powerful within him he was trying to control.

Realizing she had touched a sensitive spot, she tried

to amend by saying, "That you have a hand or not makes no difference to me."

From that position he said, "But it does make a difference to me."

He turned slowly toward her, his face closed. He tossed the hanky beside her. "I'll attend to Samisen." Abruptly, he walked out the door. A gust of cold swirled into the room and left Eithne sorry to have spoken, and almost wishing she was still mute. Amidst the escape there had been no opportunity to tell Ketha about Bron's hand. And even she wondered if her mother could heal such a wound.

She felt alone even though the old sheepdog slept before the fire. Her appetite was gone. Regret churned in the pit of her stomach. What good was a voice when she could not speak words that might ease a person's heartache. Even so, she knew Bron's wound was beyond healing with words. Then if not by words, she wondered if true love could heal deep wounds? If she loved him enough would he forget his deformity? Would he forget he could not play his harp? Nay, he would never forget. The loss would eat at him until the day he died.

She crawled under the blankets and faced the firelight. Utter weariness befell her. She heard clumping footsteps sounding through the connecting wall of the stable and Samisen's snorts. She tried very hard to keep her eyes open while she waited for Bron's return.

On the low wooden table lay a pool of light under the lamp; underneath, on a woolen hearth rug the old sheepdog shifted every now and again. She listened to his breathing.

Once a tiny scratchy sound came from a corner of the cupboard—a wee mouse. The sheepdog lifted his head and watched the mouse reproachfully, then over to Eithne, as if to say he could not be expected to do a cat's work. The mouse disappeared and all was quiet again.

Eithne woke at intervals all through the night. Bron did not return and she suspected he slept in the stable straw with Samisen.

When she stirred, the old sheepdog stirred as well. He got up slowly from before the fire and came across and stood a moment by Eithne's bed and dropped a friendly cool nose into her hand, lying open on the bed. It felt like a reassurance to Eithne that all was well. Then he walked back to the rug and flopped down with a long sigh.

All night long upon the hearth, the soft trail of smoke rose from the peat, slowly and steadily weaving the endless mystery of night and dreaming.

Next day, Eithne awoke to the smell of scones and a whistling teakettle. Hunger gripped her and before she attempted her absolutions, she ate three scones one right after the other. A fourth she fed to the dog and let him out the door into the gray light of morning.

Her throat hurt and she attempted to soothe it by drinking warm tea, but she knew the truth of it. Sheelin was pulling her voice from her little by little and with it would eventually go her very essence. It frightened her and she wished Bron was at her side, holding her in his strong arms.

She rose from the table and searched through the trunk for more clothing. She found a woolen hooded cape the deep green of yew leaves. She also found a pair of sealskin boots that she pulled upon her feet. Once dressed, she went outside and around to the stable at the croft's rear. The door was already open and she peered inside, but discovered it to be empty.

She felt abandoned and tears glazed her eyes. Where had he gone? Would he come back? She turned and scanned the landscape. Under the vast sky was nothing but rocks and more rocks, rising and falling in and about the surrounding bogs. Even the swans were not in sight. Alas, she decided to go in search of Gibbers. Obnoxious as he was, he might prove to be her only companion. As she stepped round to the croft's front, the old sheepdog padded up to her and with ears down and tail switching she knew she had one more friend.

Off she went, her cape flowing about her ankles. The air was fresh and as she breathed in deeply her head cleared and her sorriness dissipated. The turf was wet and squelchy under her feet and once she ended up to her knee in bog and almost lost her boot. After that the dog took the lead and she gladly followed its more canny trail over the land. Now she did not fear losing her way for she sensed the dog would lead her just as safely to the croft. She felt somewhat adventurous, especially when she came over a rise and saw the sea.

The dog ferreted out the easiest path down the wet dark cliffs and guided her to the mouth of an arching sea cave. Outside on the ledges broken driftwood lay splintered, and dead dogfish lay strewn about. Ever curious, she stepped inside. There was a deep lake inside, and seaweed hung limp and clammy and dark from the walls. It felt a queer and even dangerous place—her feet slipped on the treacherous weed, and she flung her arms upward, clutching against the rock. Her hands sank wrist-deep under the green slimy weed, and her fingers closed around a thick strong iron mooring ring. It had been driven into the rock. It was rusted and hung hidden by the dripping weeds.

The dog had run into the rear of the cave and began to bark. Eithne heard a woman's chastening voice and saw a bevy of small stones rain through the air, pelting the head of the dog.

"Who has come?" came a bold voice. *Who has come . . . who has come?* sounded again and again in an echoing reverberation of the cave.

"'Tis I," announced Eithne, and her own voice filled the cave with echoing. *I . . . I . . . I.*

She heard a splash and squinted down into the dark blue-green waters of the sea cave lake. Suddenly, right before her a woman's golden head rose out of the water.

"And who is 'I'?" she asked.

Eithne did not immediately speak for she was in the midst of surprise. The woman was a mermaid. Her golden hair fell in a flowing tangle of seaweed and tiny shells about her shoulders. At her throat was a starfish on a pearl string choker.

"I am Eithne," she volunteered, and then too late thought it might not be wise to tell her name.

"And who is Eithne?" the mermaid asked, her eyes bright and blue as heaven.

"I've come to the island with a sea clansman."

"Who is the sea clansman?" demanded the mermaid.

Eithne saw no harm in saying, "Bron mac Llyr."

Upon hearing this, the mermaid's face lifted and she said, "Bron mac Llyr, you say?"

"Aye, that . . . is . . . who . . . I . . . said." Eithne tried to speak soft and slow to stop the echoing.

The mermaid turned and floated upon her back, a slow grin upon her lips. Her tail was a silver scaled shimmer and Eithne felt the urge to tell her she was beautiful. But at the moment the mermaid seemed quite uninterested in what she might think.

"Who are you?" Eithne finally asked.

Her attention refocused on Eithne and she said, "I am Sarenn." And with a flip of her fin, she gave Eithne a drenching and disappeared under the water.

'Twas rude, thought Eithne, wiping the cold droplets from her face.

The dog came over and nosed her hand sympathetically. "Aye, friend, there's no accounting for others' bad manners." She sighed, rubbing his furry head.

Watching the water creeping about her feet, she said, "Beway, the tide is rising and we best leave the cave and climb to higher ground. Maybe we will return another day, and maybe not. I should bring Gibbers. Sarenn and he might make great companions."

She found herself not only chattering but singing away as she climbed up the cliffs. It had been so long since she could freely speak that the overflow bubbled out of her mouth like a new discovered wellspring.

That is how Bron came upon her as she and the dog skirted the cliffs. He was riding Samisen. He slipped off and leading the horse walked toward her.

She smiled fully. He appeared very bold and handsome. She did not miss that he still held the illusion of his hand. His own cape and his mass of long black hair flapped in the rising wind. She loved him she knew, but she was not sure if it was the true love of which he spoke and longed for.

He embraced her and said, "I was worried. When I returned you were gone."

She drew back and looked at him, her eyes sparkling with relief. "I was trying to find you as well. You left me without a word."

"Do not blame yourself. 'Twas my own foul mood and confusion. Though I am glad to return to these Blessed Isles. All has changed within me. I am not the man who left."

"Then who are you?" Eithne asked gently.

Bron dropped his arms from her and turned away. For a long time he stared out to the sea and then he slowly shook his head in quandary. Turning to face Eithne, he said, "I do not know."

She stepped toward him and wrapped her arms around the barrel of his broad chest. Her cheek pressed against him, she said, "Who are any of us? I do not know. Am I swan or woman? Gibbers tells me I am an 'undesarvin', wicked gurrul'."

"Do you believe it?"

"I used to. Then when you loved me"—her voice quivered with emotion—"I knew it was not so. I thought to myself if a man like Bron mac Llyr loves me, then I must not be so 'undesarvin', and if I could in turn love him, I was not such a 'wicked gurrul'. 'Tis simple enough."

"And do you love me, Eithne?"

She looked up at him, seeing the fine lines trailing from the corners of his gemstone eyes; seeing the roughness and softness beneath the stubble of black beard.

"Aye, I love you. Why do you ask? Yesterday, I broke my silence to speak it. So soon do you doubt me?"

"Arrah . . ." He sighed deeply. "'Tis myself I doubt, not you." His arms tightened around her and his lips kissed the crown of her head. "I fear, Eithne. I've been a hypocrite. I fear more than love."

Eithne's heart sunk. "You do not love me?"

"Oh . . . nay . . . do not think that!" His breath, a defeated exhalation, stirred the strands of hair on her forehead. "Without my hand, I have nothing to offer you. I fear your love, because I am not worthy of it. I cannot accept that I will never play my harp again . . . that I will never ride to battle with my clansmen. A man of the sea needs two hands to toss and gather his fishnet, to row his boat. I am no true man for you. All this brings me grief."

A frown gathered on Eithne's face. "Let go of it. You are more than man enough for me."

With the utterance of this illumination, silence fell between them. She held him and he her, a pair of shadows in the chastening wind. As she stood on the cliffs above the sea in his strong embrace, she wondered why men thought as they did.

After a time, he released her. He touched his mouth in an assuring kiss to her forehead. "Look, the sun peers out from behind the clouds."

She gave him a hopeful smile, "Aye, I would welcome the sun's warmth."

"Come, then," he invited. "I can hardly wait to share my island with you."

"Your island?"

"Aye, 'tis my birthright. Here I was born and here I hope to die."

Leaving Samisen to find his own way, Bron caught her fingers in his own and, hand in hand, they set off together to explore.

"Does anyone else live here besides yourself?"

"No one."

"Are you sure?"

"Did you meet someone?"

"I did. In the cave below. I met a mermaid named Sarenn."

A curious sparkle filled his eyes and he laughed outright. "Sarenn!"

"Aye, Sarenn," said Eithne, feeling a pang of jealousy. 'Twas no small pang either. It was enough to cause her to wish she'd repaid Sarenn's rudeness with a little of her own.

His head lifted. "There. See?" He pointed to the nearby headland. "See the circle of standing stones? 'Tis like your own outside Rath Morna."

Eithne looked, but she did so halfheartedly. She thought he was trying to distract her from questioning him more about Sarenn, and indeed she did have questions.

His pace hastened against the buffeting of the peat-scented wind. The turf was wet underfoot and Eithne's toes were getting colder with each step.

"'Tis a hallowed circle of stones from where the spirits of my clansmen set sail along the sea-road of the dead. These are the most ancient rocks on earth. When we come nearer you'll hear them speak. Within these stones as a child I learned to hear the voice of silence. Here spirit takes on form and form is hidden in spirit."

The tall stones flashed in the sunlight like polished obelisks. Gray and striated with whirling loops of darker and lighter gray with white spots, each seemed like the endless circles of heaven. When Eithne stepped within its boundary, she immediately felt the undying throb of life itself.

Here the buffeting winds did not enter. She stood still and breathed in the gold of sunlight, the silence of stone, the pulse of the sea, and the smell of earth. Ketha's words returned to her: "There is another world. It is hidden in this one." In this moment she had found the other world.

The lilting sounds of a harp rippled the air. She turned her head this way and that to see from where the music came, but it came from nowhere.

Across from her Bron laughed. "'Tis the fairy folk of Tir nan Og. Come dance the dance of love with me, milady."

Delight fountained through Eithne. She did not hang back when his strong arm circled her waist. Stepping toe-to-toe, they moved together, she with willowy languor and he with lightness of foot. Their feet traced patterns over the soft mossy earth and through space and air. Around and around, turning nimbly with springing steps, he caught her close to him. Their dancing became a brilliant, sweet harmony of sound, spirit, and motion. He lifted her high over his head and whirled her until she near swooned with dizziness. Life pulsed into her and the landscape glimmered with aliveness. The harp music began to fade and again the pulse of silence reigned within the stone circle.

Amid his laughter he dropped her gently upon the springy turf and collapsed beside her. When their eyes met they met fiercely.

Breasts heaving with breathlessness Eithne asked, "And do you know who you are now, Bron mac Llyr?"

"Aye, now I am your lover." He sat back on his heels. One-handed, he stripped off his cloak and then, his tunic. His torso was lean, all muscle and bone. He loosened the lacings that held his braces and stepped out of them. Eithne's senses raced, seeing the arching prow of his manhood tumescent with desire. Naked and virile, he came beside her.

Eithne's face flushed at his boldness, yet inwardly she burned with a matching desire.

He brought her hand to his lips, turned it, and kissed the palm. She exhaled slowly, sinking farther into the soft earth at her back. Aligning his long length against hers, he lowered his head to her own and kissed her lips. The kiss raced through her flesh like fire. Her nipples began to tingle and lower; between her thighs, the hollow of her womb ached for filling.

He reached to undo her cloak and the shoulder ties

of her gown and slipped it over her breasts and down off her hips so she lay naked before him. On her skin danced the warming rays of sunlight and inside she felt the gush of her own heat.

"You are very beautiful, my swan witch." His voice was soft with passion.

"I feel so beneath your gaze. Your eyes say it . . . as does your heart. I love you, Bron mac Llyr. I will love no other but you. I will sing my love lilt to no other but you and we shall be bonded together as long as the fates so will. My words can now be spoken. My power is to open. My promise can never be broken."

And upon the silence fell the sweet shimmer of Eithne's voice upraised in song. The lilt of ecstasy was in her singing, and the gift of heart, and the promise of love whose true face is rarely seen.

In Bron's emerald eyes Eithne saw moisture glitter. A slow delicious sweep of memory brought to her mind that first night of lovemaking between them. She reached to him and touched his cheek.

"Between us weaves the thread of seasons. I love you beyond all reason," she sang softly.

She brushed aside the tangle of his long black hair and smoothed the fine lines that life and battle had graven into his brow. Where fingers had gone, lips could follow. Moving from brow to eyelids, down sculpted cheeks to lips that welcomed her own like a thirsty man in a barren land.

Drawing away from his lips she whispered, "Everything lost is found again. Everything hurt is healed in the end."

The power of her love was filling her like a thousand blessings. She kissed his face and throat, lowered her face down to touch her mouth upon his shoulders and muscled chest. When her lips touched his nipples he moaned, and his arms went around her. She moved her head lower and her tongue traced the dark hairy furrow of his belly. Her breasts brushed against the bent bow of his manhood.

With heart and flesh she worshiped him from head to foot, adoring him, restoring him, invoking his passion. She could not withhold herself. And soon, his urgency met her own and he rolled her over onto the soft earth and claimed her mouth with a hard thrusting tongue. His fingers slipped gently between her thighs. She readily opened to his hands and all power of motion left her limbs, all awareness seemed centered toward the sweetness he was awakening in the hidden wellspring of her body. She arched to him and he mounted her. She felt his weight as his hard rod blazed into the secret space of her essence. He gripped her hips and she felt a rush of power. She pulled him against her, wanting all.

Not only was the power of love between them awakened, so was the power of the stones that flowed up from the earth beneath them. The warmth in the joining turned to fire. Eithne trembled as the fire moved upward, setting new fires in her belly and beneath her ribs, up to her crown where the very heavens seemed to burst open.

Moans escaped from her throat as his thrusts quickened with the ancient throb of earth and sea. He came like a great, swelling wave, crashing upon the ragged cliffs of Tir nan Og. In that instant, their eyes found each other in a joining of infinity.

She transformed into a swan, winging on to ecstasy . . . and then she was woman once again . . . full-fleshed, full-bodied with spirit free.

His eyes hooded, his mouth hovered above hers and her gaze fell into his green-fire depths. With heart-expanding slowness, she lingered in the radiance of their connection. His skin held the flush of erotic warmth and was moistly hot against her own. She felt his thoughts, his feelings, and his love.

"Aye," she breathed softly. "Is this the true loving you told me of?"

He shifted and without breaking their connection, rolled to his back and cradled her gently in his arms. He stroked her hair and looked a long deep moment into her eyes.

"'Tis that, my swan witch." He kissed her forehead and tightened his embrace.

His face held serenity. She'd not seen him so at peace before. Her gaze lowered to his sword hand.

The illusion was gone.

Had he at last accepted himself as he was? Aye, she sensed he had. And she loved him all the more for it.

Chapter

12

Standing on the cliffs, Eithne and Bron watched the sun sink into the sea in a welter of crimson and gold. From below they heard the waves crash and suck against the stones. With mewling cries, seabirds swooped and dove into the dark waters. A stiff breeze was whipping up the gray clouded sky, bringing the threat of rain. Eithne snuggled closer to Bron, shivering slightly. Gently, he caressed her hair and kissed the top of her head.

"Are you cold, my swan witch?"

She shook her head. "Nay . . . a feeling. I dreamed of Sheelin last night." She turned and faced Bron, gazing up at him from wide eyes that glistened with unshed tears. "Bron, I'm afraid."

His embrace tightened. "There is no need to be, you are here with me and safe."

She ran her long fingers through his loose black hair, feeling it flow like raw silk in her hands. "I grow weaker each day. I do not only fear for myself but for you and your clansmen."

"What did you see in your dream?" he asked gravely.

"Sheelin came here, to Tir nan Og. With him was a host of warriors. They appeared to be both man and beast . . . like those you told me of who cut off your hand."

"Fomorians." His voice held hardness. "'Tis not surprising to me he has found an ally in them."

"How are we to stop him?"

"Do not fear. Neither Sheelin nor Fomorian will be able to harm you."

Eithne sighed. "I wish that could be so . . . but I cannot believe it. Sheelin will rule Myr. Since my childhood he has plotted to that end. And now I fear he comes to Tir nan Og. Because of me, you and your clansmen will suffer. I have brought you nothing but trouble."

Bron held her tightly. "No, never think that. You have brought me love." He kissed her with a passion that matched the crashing of the waves against the wild, windswept cliffs of Tir nan Og.

Her breathing deepened. Her lips moved under his with the desperateness of her need for his love and his protection. She leaned into his body, absorbing the hard structure of his hips, all of her clinging to his strength and presence. When his lips drew away, she pressed her cheek against his broad chest and held him close.

She would have been content to spend the rest of her days in that embrace, but his attention suddenly shifted.

"There is a curragh approaching," he said, turning

her away from him and to the sea. "It's running contrary to both tide and wind."

"Who could it be?" She squinted.

"It's hard to tell in this light. But I will guess 'tis my father, the sea king. Only he could sail his Wave Sweeper so against the elements."

The sail dropped and yet no oars hit the water, but still the curragh came on, beaching itself with the scrap of hardened timbers.

In the twilight, Eithne could see it was a small boat, but ornately carved with lines of blue fire that splayed out from the dolphin figurehead. Three figures disembarked and began moving up the beach. Single file they began climbing a cliff path.

"Aye," said Bron, an expectant light in his eyes. "'Tis father, his man, Drunn, and the Lady Niamh. Let us meet them."

His hand at her waist, Bron pressed Eithne forward. Reluctantly, she moved in step with him. The wind seemed cooler and she drew her cloak closely around her. Slowly the trio made their way up the hill.

"Arrah! Manannan mac Llyr," he shouted out as they approached. Then he was in a full arm embrace with his father. Eithne remained reserved. In the graying light she met the kindly gaze of the Lady Niamh.

She was young, maybe younger than Eithne herself. Her face was thin, with eyes more gray than green and hair nearing the golden shades of sunrise. When Bron moved from his father to embrace Niamh, Eithne felt uneasy with possessiveness. She begrudged the other women in Bron's life. Surely, they all loved and wanted him as she did . . . and she was in no mind to share.

The man, Drunn, received a slap upon the back from Bron and a great flashing smile. Eithne noticed that Bron's cape discreetly covered his sword arm through the greetings.

"I would have you meet my Lady Eithne," said Bron, stepping back to include her.

That he had spoken "my" rather than "the" Lady Eithne before her name put to rest some of Eithne's apprehensions, but not all. How long would she be his lady? The sea king did not appear as though he would relish a gaggle of swanlings to bounce upon his knee as his grandchildren.

He was appraising her . . . even as she took his measure. The fading light shadowed the lines of his noble features and danced from the gold work of the royal circlet that held his long black hair.

"Lady Eithne." He bowed, ever so slightly. Beside him, the Lady Niamh curtsied gracefully. Out of insolence, Eithne had refused to participate in the false courtly graces of Rath Morna . . . so she knew not what to do. Should she curtsy or bow? Should she speak a proclamation of fealty to this king? She knew not . . . so she did naught, but give a slight nod of her head.

"Come, then," said Bron putting his arm around her waist. "A gale is brewing. Let us seek shelter."

The sea king was standing with his back to the fire. Bron had hooked his foot around a stool and pulled it over to the hearth. Eithne slipped off her cape and began pouring up hot cups of tea. She knelt down beside Bron and with tongs snatched up buttery scones from the pan to serve to the others. Bron had not taken off his cape and was careful to move discreetly about, never exposing his sword arm to full view.

The Lady Niamh sat shyly upon the edge of the bed. The man, Drunn, seated himself on the hearth rug and scratched the old dog's ears.

"So!" began the sea king. "I believed you as good as dead, after Carrowmore. 'Twas rumored the Fomorians captured you as they fled the field."

Eithne offered him a mug of tea. He took deep gulps and set the cup aside, continuing, "Two days ago, I was fishing and that merhag Sarenn popped her head up out of the sea and told me you had returned to Tir nan Og. I came to see for myself."

"And so you've seen," said Bron quietly.

Eithne stole a glance at Bron's face. It was immutable. He could not forever hide his deformity from his father. When would he speak the truth?

"Why did you not send word to me?" asked the sea king.

She saw the slight gather of tension in Bron's well-formed shoulders. Suddenly, he stood up. He threw his cloak to one side, held up the nub of his sword arm, and faced his father.

For long moments the room was so silent Eithne could hear the flames eating away at the dried peat. Her heart ached for him.

The sea king stood with arms folded, his eye steady on his son as if he did not see his handless arm.

Then Bron himself broke the silence. "I was as good as dead without my sword hand."

The sea king uttered an oath that startled even Lady Niamh on the bedside. "Arrah! By all the gods of earth and sea, you are a fool to think it! A man is not a hand or foot." He stepped forward and drew Bron into the large oval of his arms. In an unrestrained show of tenderness and love, he cried aloud, "You live, my son. You live!"

The moment became a time of renewing bonds, and then for smiling. When Bron released his father they were both smiling.

"Let us eat and rejoice in the living," said the sea king. His gaze shifted to Eithne and she hastily lowered her eyes and released the breath she was holding in one full sigh. "Spread the table, milady, we will feast."

"I'm not so sure that scones and tea are much of a feast, Milord Mac Llyr," she openly declared.

"Aye, then, see yonder." He pointed. The man, Drunn, began to unwrap a bundle he'd carried up from the curragh. A great silvery- and black-finned fish was revealed. "Niamh, put it on the fire spit."

Niamh jumped up and was at it faster than Eithne thought possible. Soon, the smell of roasting fish filled the croft. In no time at all the four sat themselves around the table and set their appetites to scones and succulent sweet roasted white fish.

During the meal there was hardly a word of conversation. Often, Eithne looked to Bron and found assurance in his gaze. His demeanor had lightened. How could he have believed his father and clansmen would shun him? His father loved him. There was no mistaking it. Manannan mac Llyr held all the qualities that she wished for in her own father. He radiated power and patience, strength and tenderness. She sensed no avarice in him.

Later, after eating, while Bron, Drunn, and the sea king spoke of the battle of Carrowmore, Eithne sat with Niamh before the hearth roasting hazelnuts.

"'Tis my place to say that you may encounter the Fomorians sooner than you had wished."

Overhearing Bron speak this, Eithne turned to the three men who still sat at the table.

Drunn shrugged. "I would welcome the opportunity."

The sea king was less enthused. "Why say you this?" The firelight painted his concerned thin features in sharp angles and planes.

Bron caught the gravity in Manannan's eye and clarified. "For want of greater power, my Lady Eithne's father, the sorcerer Sheelin, may now be forming an alliance with the Fomorians."

"How would that involve the sea clans?" asked Manannan, looking at Bron.

"His object is to invade the land of Myr."

"Arrah!" breathed Manannan. "I did not think that possible. In Myr dwell the swan sister clans who hold the last vestige of old earth and the powers of transformation. How could he, a man, invade Myr?"

"Through the power of the singer's voice that he even now usurps from his own daughter, Eithne."

Manannan's gaze riveted to Eithne. She quickly lowered her own under the sheer shock of his surprise.

She thought, now he knows his son loves a woman not of his kith. He will surely despise me. Stealing a glance at Niamh's impassive face, she wondered how this news would be taken by her and the others of their clan.

She listened as Bron's soft words further enlightened the sea king. "Eithne's mother is Ketha, the swan sister and healer. Sheelin has kept her imprisoned for many years. Now Ketha is free and has returned to Myr, but Eithne cannot. If Eithne enters Myr it will enable Sheelin with his Unseelie Court to follow. Even now, he drains her essence and attempts to take upon himself her singer's voice."

The sea king scratched his chin with irritation. "I will not ask how you became the lady's champion, but you must answer true whatever I ask."

"I will," pledged Bron.

"How do you know the sorcerer is coming here?"

"Eithne dreamed so," replied Bron, his eyes unwavering from his father.

"Arrah," he muttered gravely. "On first tide, Drunn and I will take word to our other clansmen to gather here at Tir nan Og." He shifted upon his seat and turned his attention toward the Lady Niamh. "How soon, Niamh? How long do we have to prepare?"

Remaining motionless herself, Eithne's gaze went to Niamh. She seemed more the pixie than the seeress as she chewed on the roasted mush of a hazelnut. "Not long. The rising gale is the portent."

The sea king met eyes with Eithne and spoke pointedly. "I swear by my sword, the Answerer, Lady Eithne, to protect you from all harm. It will strike in your defense and shield you from all blows. Your enemies are now mine and my clan's."

"Thank you, milord," breathed Eithne in a most grateful voice. She looked to Bron but his own gaze was locked upon his maimed sword arm. Her heart sank, knowing that he was cursing the fates that brought his father and not him to stand as her defender.

The sea king turned back to Bron and Drunn. Eithne listened as during the passing hour, in low voices, they conspired in plan making.

It was very warm before the fire. She wiped her brow and with tongs snatched out the smoking hazelnuts off the nest of peat. Once there was a loud pop and a nut jumped out of the fire onto the hearth.

Niamh giggled. "At home we put two nuts side by side in the fire and if they remain where you put them that means you and your lover will never be parted. Shall I do it for you?"

Eithne felt uneasy with such divinations . . . because they never worked in her favor. Before she could protest, Niamh had in hand two hazelnuts and set them together on the smoldering peat.

A little anxious, she watched the pair of nuts roast quietly. She started when she felt the sudden touch of Bron's hand upon her shoulder.

He chuckled. "Why are you staring so intently into the fire?"

"We are seeing if she and her lover will ever be parted," volunteered Niamh.

"'Tis no question to ask a pair of nuts," said Bron, a touch of scolding in his voice. Amidst Niamh's protests, and with a quick twitch of the tongs, he had the nuts out of the fire and on the gray stone hearth. He picked up one nut and gave it to Eithne with the request "Will you peel it for me?"

She watched him smile and felt relief. She did not want to know the future between them either. "Aye, milord."

She peeled it and tossed the black bits into the fire. With her fingers, she offered the hot sweet mealiness of the nut to his lips. His tongue tip brushed her fingers pads teasingly, before his teeth bit into the nut meat.

He chewed, swallowed, and said, "More."

"Well," said Niamh lightly. "I see you have already found the advantage in being a one-handed man."

Eithne turned hastily to Bron to see if her remark caused offense. His features remained softened with tolerance.

He sighed forlornly. "Believe me, my sister, when I say there is no advantage."

Looking from Bron to Niamh, Eithne's vision expanded and she saw clearly the kinship between the two. She should have realized it sooner . . . that Niamh was his younger sister. There was no point in being jealous of his sister. The part of her who always wished for a true friend of her own, and had no one but Gibbers, relaxed and warmed to Niamh.

"I myself am ready for sleep," the sea king said, rising to his feet. "Niamh, you share the bed with Lady Eithne. The three of us will sleep in the stable."

Drunn stood as well. Eithne exchanged a disappointed glance with Bron. She did not want to spend even a single night out of his arms. He must have read the message of her eyes and clearly felt the longing of her heart.

"'Tis but one night, milady," he whispered to her ear. He kissed her cheek and then came to his feet. "I'll be but a shout away . . . through the connecting wall with the stable." It seemed she might melt under the compassion of his eyes. His parting smile was an endearment.

"Deep peace to you," said the sea king as he led the other two men out into the dark night.

A cold gust touched Eithne's neck as the door shut.

"Aye, a fierce gale is brewing," said Niamh, stepping to secure the door more tightly. "Put more peat on the fire and let's be to bed."

When Eithne pulled back the blankets to crawl into the bed, Niamh was still sitting on the edge combing out her hair. "Can I do that for you?" asked Eithne, surprising herself. Her hair was so beautiful.

The lamplight reflected over the smooth curve of Niamh's narrow shoulder, leaving her face in shadow. "Aye, you can . . . and thank you. I am called Niamh of the Golden Hair. 'Tis my pride."

Niamh gave her the comb.

Outside, the wind moaned like a lonely and frightened child. Something loose tapped and scraped against the door as if a lost soul begged safe haven in the wildness of the stormy night. The old sheepdog lifted his head and growled halfheartedly at the door and then returned to dozing.

"There are many likenesses between you and your brother, Bron," began Eithne carefully.

"True, but we have different mothers. I am much younger than he. Did he tell you of us?"

"No," said Eithne.

"I suspected it. He is close-mouthed in some ways. Do you love him?"

"Aye," Eithne said plainly, continuing to comb through the silky tangles of her hair.

"You must know you are not alone in loving him."

"Aye," relinquished Eithne with resignation.

"Yet, you are the first he has called 'his lady.' I think that is significant. Don't you?"

"I don't know what to think. He is your brother and you know him well." She felt a little defeated by Niamh's insights.

"True, but not well enough. How does he compare to the other men you have loved?"

Eithne smiled to herself. There was something humorous about Niamh's questions. No doubt she was a clever girl. She felt quite inexperienced in comparison. She could not compare Bron to other men because there had been none . . . except those her father had beheaded. She would not tell this to Niamh.

"He is the first man I have ever loved," she confessed honestly. "I'm not so experienced as he in loving."

"You need not be." Niamh turned about and sat with her arms clasped around her knees. Putting the comb aside, Eithne pulled back the blankets and crawled under them. Her mind was brimming with more questions.

"Why do you say that?"

"I say it because I know it." Niamh slipped under the blankets beside Eithne. "Men like to be all-knowing in matters of love. If you are more knowledgeable it is to your discredit."

"Why?"

"I have wondered that very thing myself."

"And?" prompted Eithne.

"And I don't know why. 'Tis the way of things."

Snuggling under the covers, Eithne said, "You know what I think? I think no one knows anything about love. They just pretend to. Bron tells me everyone seeks true love but they never find it. He says, 'The secret is to love more than to fear.'"

Niamh raised herself on one elbow and asked Eithne, "He told you that?"

"Aye."

"I must say 'tis very wise. I did not know my brother to be so wise."

"Aye." Eithne smiled cannily. "The world can be full of surprises."

Their eyes met in a mutual exchange of amusement. Then Niamh fell back onto her pillow and her ringing laughter mingled with the whistling of the wind.

Chapter

13

Eithne's sleep was full of nightmares. A part of her knew she dreamed, but that was no consolation as she lay in the paralysis of fear's phantoms. She woke often, finding comfort in the faint flicker of flame spreading outward from the hearth and the steady breathing of Niamh beside her. Outside, the wind moaned and whispered like the ghosts of her dreams. Her eyelids felt heavy. She was afraid to close them because as soon as she did the frightening images of her dreams returned.

In the gray light of morning she roused from the dark clouds of a fitful sleep. She heard a tapping at the door.

"Musha! 'Tisss cold asss cursesss," came a faint, hissing voice.

"Who's there?" grumbled Niamh as she stirred beside Eithne in the bed and shushed the old sheep-dog's growling.

Eithne knew that voice and temper anywhere. "Pay no heed. 'Tis," and then she had to swallow hard for her voice was as weak as a wisp. "'Tis Gibbers," she at last managed. Her arms and legs felt heavy as if she had never slept at all.

"And who is Gibbers?"

"Open the door and peek at your own risk," she rasped out. The inside of Eithne's throat felt like fire. She wanted water . . . all the water in the world.

Niamh had climbed from the bed and was stepping across the room to unlatch the door.

Eithne felt the gush of cold and threw off her covers to expose herself to its cool caress. Why was she so hot? The air seemed stifling.

"Begorrah and begobs! 'Tis a fine time to be commin'. Ye kape me out here the night through, an me feet al' froze."

So it hadn't been just the wind blowing the night past, realized Eithne. It had been Gibbers outside the croft moaning to come in. She faced the wall and wished he would disappear in the bogs.

Minutes later, it was Bron's voice that brought her fully around.

His voice seemed to fill the room. "I'll not have a cantankerous troll complaining before my fire. We've enough troubles . . . so keep your jaw shut or disappear into the bogs where you belong," he ordered.

"Am I to be grovelin' fur any small favors yer plazed to give?" whined Gibbers.

"Aye!" returned Bron sharply. "Make yourself scarce."

Bron looked to Eithne. She was sitting up with the bed covers clutched to her breast, her eyes meeting his like pools of fire. She said nothing, but all of her called him.

"Eithne, love! 'Tis all right—I'm here!" He crossed the room and came down on the bed beside her. He put his arms around her and she clung to him, crying softly.

Her hand on her throat, she whispered, "My voice . . ."

He touched her forehead and felt the feverishness of her skin. He turned to Niamh, "What is happening?"

Niamh came close. "As the sorcerer gathers his power she will weaken."

"Is there naught that we can do?"

"I do not know. My sense is that the connection of love between you strengthens her, but for how long . . ." She shook her head with doubt.

He felt Eithne's arms tighten around him.

"Arrah . . . I should not have left you last night." He stroked her hair. "But I'm here now."

"Stay close . . . I am afraid without you." Her voice was hauntingly muted, like a small lost child in a great cavern. "I need water. . . ."

He turned to Niamh, who stepped to the cupboard and was pouring water from a crockery pitcher into a cup. Accommodatingly, he put the cup to Eithne's lips. She grasped it with both hands and gulped thirstily.

"More," she breathed.

Niamh fetched the pitcher and poured full the cup . . . two times more.

Then gently, Bron eased her onto the pillows. Niamh gave him a cold damp cloth that he pressed to her temples, her cheeks, and her neck.

"How do you feel now?"

A fine winged brow knitted. "I am frightened."

He arranged his own features with confidence. "Och, you've naught to fear." He took her hand, and held it small and curving in his as he touched it gently to his lips. "The more you fear the greater power Sheelin has over you. Fear feeds the darkness."

Tears slipped down Eithne's cheeks. Bron wanted to bend over and kiss each one away, but he resisted. He knew she could not rely upon his strength alone. She must find that place in herself.

"Oh, Bron," she said, her voice agonizing. "I dare not even close my eyes. I fall into the darkness. 'Tis a great black pit." She fisted her hand. "In that place my heart feels hard as stone. I cannot breathe."

"'Tis because there is no love in that darkness." He raised his hand and touched the tip of her chin. "Look into my eyes, Eithne. What do you see there?"

She lifted her face to his. In her eyes he saw the swirling turmoil of her emotions. She searched his own for long moments. "I see . . . a wealth of love and gentleness." With softened focus they held each other's gaze. "What do you see in mine?" she asked.

Countless times he'd fallen into those depths. He'd glimpsed a myriad of her emotions, her anger, her joy, her sadness, but the unveiled void he saw now caused him the greatest of concern. "I see your fear," he said truthfully. "What are you so afraid of, Eithne?"

Tears coursing down her cheeks, she turned away from him. "Sheelin, I fear Sheelin and his Unseelie Court."

"I think not. For you know that is all illusion. Tell me truly what you fear."

She covered her face with her hands and began sobbing.

"Speak true, Eithne," he prompted.

Gently, he pried her hands from her face. "Look at me, Eithne," he commanded. His warmly empathic glance strayed to her trembling lower lip and to the faint vibration of the pulse on the curve of her throat.

She shook her head with refusal.

"I think, Eithne, you fear your own power. You fear your own power to love."

Her eyes flashed with desperateness. "I love you." She threw her arms around him and buried her head against his chest. "I love you," she murmured over and over.

He held her to him. Then her weeping burst out in inconsolable waves. He fought to contain his own welling of emotion. He did not doubt she loved him, but he sensed she withheld that most vulnerable part of herself. He was not sure why.

"Aye, you know how to love, but you don't know how to let yourself be loved . . . because you don't love yourself," he returned with deep-felt compassion.

"Musha!" interrupted the hissing voice of Gibbers from the corner. "An evil, wicked gurrul she be. She cud niver love." The rancor and sarcasm of Gibbers's words hung like vile bog gas in the air.

The times in Bron's life that he had fully lost his temper could be counted on the one hand he had. The slow fire of his anger rose as he carefully released

Eithne and let her fall against the pillows. He stood. In one great step he was before Gibbers, who had presence enough to crouch with innate cowardliness. He reached out his hand and picked Gibbers up by the thin thread of his green neck and he strode out the door.

Outside, he thumped him down and vented his anger, cleanly, clearly, and magnificently. "I'll not stand by and hear you speak ill of her. *You* are the evil, wicked one. *You* are the devil who cannot love. Now be gone. I have no wish to see your face again!"

Gibbers cringed and blathered in the burn of Bron's anger. He did not miss the full potency of the message. Hastily, he slithered out of sight.

When Bron returned, Niamh was holding the weeping Eithne. She turned to her brother and accused, "You've pushed her to the edge and off."

"Nay." His voice was low and assuring. "She cannot face the powers of darkness until she has faced the darkness in herself."

"And how is that to happen?"

"Through the night of fear."

"Nay! 'Tis an awesome ordeal. She has not the strength."

"She has my strength to draw upon . . . and after the night of fear her own strength will rise that she may face Sheelin."

Niamh still seemed unconvinced. She opened her mouth to speak again but Bron touched his fingers to her lips in a plea for silence. He would explain the ordeal to Eithne and she could make that decision for herself.

"Come now, my love."

Readily Eithne drew away from Niamh and reached for him. He pulled the bedding away and wrapped her in a flannel quilt and carried her to a chair by the fire, where he sat down, holding her against him.

By afternoon Eithne's spirits lifted as she regained her vitality. Niamh prepared a reviving drink of herbs for her that put the glow back into her countenance. Bron suggested he take her riding. She did not like giving up their cozy arrangement by the fire, but soon she sat upon Samisen's back, still cocooned in the safe cradle of Bron's arms.

The gale had passed and the sun shone bright. A rare, lonely beauty stretched over the island. She was happy to be out in the clarity of the day and away from the soul-shaking shadows of the night.

Samisen carried them across bog and rockery and down among the shifting blowing sand dunes of the southern shore. Long and pliant as silk before the wind, the gray marrum grass etched the dunes like thick whiskers.

"What is that sound?" asked Eithne, her ears straining to a sporadic clamor farther down the beach.

"'Tis the harping of seals," said Bron, gently nudging Samisen forward. "You can hear them talk on clear days like this, while they tend their newborn pups."

"And what do they say?"

Bron chuckled. "I'm not so certain. Niamh could tell you. She is that canny. Everything speaks to her . . . the winds, the sea, the stones, the animals."

Eithne watched the hundred or so dark shapes

wallow in the sand and flipper in and out of the waves.

"Beway." She smiled. "The wee things are a precious sight to see."

"And to feel," said Bron slipping down off Samisen. Doubling around, he caught a stray pup. Returning to Eithne, a huge grin upon his face he presented a wet, furry baby seal to her.

"Begorrah!" she said, laughing with pleasure. It sniffed and sneezed as she held its warm, wiggly softness close to her body. "Aye, I'll take it back to warm my bed this night."

"And what of me?" Bron tried to look hurt but was not so successful.

She flashed him her most audacious smile. "You shall warm not my bed, but myself."

He bowed playfully, but his voice held verity. "I am your servant to the end, milady."

She handed the pup to him saying, "I would truly keep it but it must remain with its own kith."

"Aye," he agreed, dropping the pup near a barking grande dame. Eithne wished he was not so ready to agree on that point. Would he drop her as easily to her mother's care if the time came?

He remounted Samisen and set a slow-paced walk up the beach.

"How long a ride to the croft?" she asked.

He nuzzled her neck and said lowly, "How long would you be wanting it to be?"

Her hand went up and caressed his rough cheek. "As long as the sun shines, I'm content to be out-of-doors."

"'Tis a true island woman you are, then." He kissed her hand. Eithne felt it to the very tips of her toes. In his loving company, her dark dreams disappeared and she wondered how she could have ever been frightened at all.

"I have something else I must show you."

They now climbed the headland slope crossing the squelchy, boggy terrain where the goldening mist thinned below the sun. With each breath, Eithne breathed in that gold.

"There ahead," said Bron. "Beyond is a barrow mound. A low narrow entrance leads within. 'Tis a sacred place. 'Tis a path into the underworlds."

She saw where he gestured and spied the rising mound with a stone slab opening.

"Now in seriousness we must speak, milady. There beneath the earth, myself and many of my clansmen have made the journey into the dark night of the soul. The sea clans believe that the greatest warrior is the warrior who has the courage to face himself. Until you face the darkness in yourself, Eithne, you cannot face the darkness of Sheelin."

The feelings of fear she'd thought had been banished with the clarity of the day returned. She looked away from Bron, back to the mound, saying, "I've enough darkness in my life. I've no wish to see more."

"Aye," returned Bron. "I understand you, but if you come through the night of fear, your mind will be stronger and cannot be broken by Sheelin's sorcery."

"Nay," she said firmly. "I'll not do this!"

"Why?"

With a wide open gaze she turned her face to him. "You know why. You have said it. I fear myself. I fear my own darkness. I . . . I am as evil as my father." Her voice broke and she began crying. Bron put his arms about her, but she shrugged him off. "Nay! I'm unworthy of your love. Leave me be."

Bron let fall his arms. "Sweet Eithne," he pleaded in a compassion-filled voice. "Let me love you. Let someone love you . . . especially your own self. If you cannot embrace your darkness . . . you'll not embrace mine nor anyone else's. And then you will truly be like Sheelin. Don't you see?"

"Aye," she sobbed. "I see too much. Too much!"

Silence fell between them as they rode to the croft. Once there Eithne remained outside, sitting upon a stool in the afternoon sun. Bron stayed near and groomed Samisen.

In early evening the winds rose in a whipping vengeance. Still silent, and inwardly churning like the sea in a gale, Eithne sat before the fire. Niamh cracked nuts and peeled them to eat. Wordless, she shared the white meat with Bron.

"'Tis your singing harp we need, my brother," said Niamh, her eyes on Bron's harp, which sat in the dust of one corner. Eithne thought it was unthinking of her to bring it up, but Bron seemed unoffended. He merely nodded his head.

In the hearth flames she watched the dance of light and dark. Her own inner battle reflected both flame and shadow. Why must the fate of Myr rest upon her shoulders? Why must she be the one to inherit the singer's voice? Why . . . why and why? She wrapped her arms around her legs and lay her forehead against her knees. Slowly, she rocked to and fro, stranded in the dilemma. She felt Bron's arm upon her shoulders, but it was no consolation.

Finally she said, "Aye, I'll do it. I'll willingly submit myself to the night of fear. But have no great expectation for I am no warrior."

His hand moved to caress her face. "Arrah," he said in a pride filled voice. "You are more warrior than has ever been seen in these Blessed Isles. You are a warrior of the heart." In a welter of tender emotion, he kissed her lightly on the lips.

And then they heard it. A haunting cry that cut through the night like a knife through flesh. The sound was brittle with pain and anguish and an incredible despair.

"What was that?" Eithne whispered. She did not miss the look exchanged between Bron and Niamh.

"It's the wind coming in off the sea," said Bron. His arm tightened around her shoulders.

Suddenly, the door blew open.

Niamh screamed as the candles blew out and the croft was plunged into darkness. In the dimness, Eithne caught the flash of white cloaks. Bron rose swiftly and walked over to face three strange women on the threshold.

"May we enter?" asked one. The flickering light from the hearth danced over the deep shadows and hollows of her thin face, giving it an almost skull-like appearance.

"Who are you?" asked Bron suspiciously.

"We've come from the spring fed pool, just beyond," said one whose hair was near silver in whiteness.

It was Eithne who recognized them. "Ask them in, Bron. They are the swan sisters who came with us at my mother's bidding."

"Aye," said Bron, with comprehension. "Forgive me."

The women stepped inside. Niamh moved to close the door against the bitter wind and quickly lit the candles.

"I am Epona of Myr," said the tallest woman, whose strongly marked features took on an austere splendor in the firelight. "These are my sisters, Ceith and Terwen. With your permission we've come to cast a circle of protection. The gale brings the harbingers of dark sorcery to Tir nan Og."

Again they heard it.

It was a wailing scream of anguish that rose and fell like a rabid wolf at midnight. It grated along bone and nerves, setting teeth on edge and fine hair on end. It drew forth the primeval fear of the night, the dead and the undead, the unembodied entities that wandered in the darkness.

Eithne had risen to her feet. She felt the blood draining from her face and her heart pacing with fear. "Aye," she said. "'Tis welcome you are to cast your circle."

"Do not be afraid, Eithne," soothed Epona. "It is your father's dark work. He thinks to frighten us all with his phantoms."

"Come, drink hot tea and sit before the fire," invited Niamh.

"Aye," echoed Bron, moving low stools and a chair for them to sit upon.

Eithne studied the swan sisters closely. She was very curious about her kinswomen. Ceith's hair was flaxen, soft, and fine; it was a halo in the candlelight. Her eyes were wide and tilted and, at that moment, reflecting the clearest blue. Terwen in contrast had blue-black hair and skin as snowy white as a dove's underwing.

"Is it true only those of pure heart can enter Myr?" asked Niamh as she offered them steaming cups of tea.

Terwen looked over at Ceith. Eithne could not read the glance that passed between them. Epona smiled into her cup, and said, "That is the tradition."

"More than anything I wish to one day see Myr," said Eithne. "Is it so different from here?"

"Very much so," assured Epona, not elaborating.

The death-wail came again. This time it was nearer. The cry drifted across the night and faded on the wind. A lull fell in the conversation and brought the true errand of the visit to point.

Setting her cup aside, Epona said, "Let us now cast the circle." She reached over and touched Eithne on the arm gently. "Eithne, you are of our kith. You shall help us."

Me? Eithne almost asked aloud, unsure that she had heard Epona's words correctly. As if fully aware of Eithne's self-doubt, Epona nodded her head affirming her request. Eithne felt sudden pride and for the first time in her life, a sense of belonging. Her gaze met Bron's and he gave her a supportive smile.

"Ceith, move the stools, and Eithne, build up the fire," directed Epona.

Eithne hurried to obey her while she bent to the hearth, watching Epona from the corners of her eyes.

Epona removed her feather cloak and laid it aside. She unfastened a large pouch from about her waist and took from it two smaller silk bags, and four white, long wing feathers.

The fresh peat that Eithne had laid across the smoldering fire caught hold. From one bag Epona took a handful of mixed herbs and scattered it on the fire. Heavy curls of smoke circled above the fire like coiling serpents. Eithne sneezed. The scent was sharp and made her nose tingle.

"Now let us join arms together, sisters, and cast the circle of protection," said Epona.

Silently, Eithne and the other swan sisters interlaced their arms. In unison their voices rose in a soft chant, pouring out from their hearts in low flowing rhythm. Eithne found herself singing for the first time odd patterns of sound that instinctively flowed from her lips. On one level she knew that innate knowledge of the chants was her birthright as a swan maiden. Three times she and the others slowly circled moonwise within the croft.

Then, Epona raised the white swan feathers above her head and waved them through the air saying, "We banish from this croft all things dark and mischievous. We call forth the circle of light and protection around us."

She lowered her hand. She held the feathers splayed before her, took one to herself, and said, "Earth witch, ear to the ground."

Then she faced Ceith and said, "Water witch, arms in the stream." Ceith's long graceful fingers took the feather from her hand.

She turned to Terwen. "Fire witch, breath to the flame." Terwen clasped her feather.

Lastly, Epona met Eithne's eyes. "Swan witch, throat full of song." Her fingertips trembled as she touched the feather tip. Then, like a spark of goodness, Eithne felt well-being enfold her.

"Take these feathers and place them in a corner of the croft to unite the four winds in protection," instructed Epona.

Eithne moved past the other women to the corner nearest where Bron sat. There she secured the feather high up, between the chinks of stone. Then she returned to center and intertwined her arms with those of her sisters before the hearth fire.

Epona began humming and tossed a red powder onto the fire. Flames flared and flashed with bright sparks, their light banishing the shadows, and darkness fluttered on black wings from the croft.

Epona closed her eyes and took a deep breath, and then spoke softly. "The circle is cast and sealed in place."

Eithne looked immediately to Bron. There was light in his eyes and he matched her gaze with much warmth.

Abruptly, Epona said, "We must leave now."

"So soon?" said Eithne, turning her attention to the

swan sisters. She hoped to speak more with them of Myr and the sisterhood.

"Aye, my child," she said, picking up her beautiful feathered cloak and placing it over her shoulders. "There is much left undone."

"'Tis not a night that I would wish to be out-of-doors," observed Niamh. "You are welcome here."

"Our thanks to you." Ceith smiled. "But out-of-doors is more to our liking."

And with that Terwen opened the door and the three women disappeared into the darkness as if they had never been.

Chapter
14

It was after midday when eight curraghs beached on the rough sands of the western shore. The sun had burned away the last clouds of morning mist and the air was heavy and thick with the smell of the sea and the shrill cries of the gulls.

Eithne sat upon Samisen on the cliffs above watching Bron greet his father, Drunn, and other clansmen. The tall figures moved through the foaming shallows to the drier upper reaches of the rocky beach. She counted twenty and six warriors. Like Bron their hair was waist long, thick, and as black as night's darkest hour. The sunlight reflected off their armor gold and bronze, and struck like fire from their dolphin emblemed shields. Their swords were sheathed and their spears held upright.

Filled with nervousness, she patted Samisen's neck and thought to herself, *These men have left their women and homes to come here to face a terrible evil. And what my part will be I do not know. I am weakness itself in the face of their strength.*

As they approached, Eithne attempted to compose her features with self-possession, but she was far from it.

"My Lady Eithne," introduced Bron simply. One or two clansmen gave her a half nod and the others hardly gave her a glance. Bron took the bridle reins in his hand and turned Samisen's head to follow him as he walked beside his clansmen.

"The lady has agreed to submit to the ordeal," said Bron to his father.

"Arrah!" voiced the sea king, approvingly. He met Eithne with a respectful eye. "Tonight?"

"Aye," said Bron. "Tonight. The sooner the better. Sheelin will come. Since you have left each night the winds blow stronger as he gathers the dark forces."

"There is much treachery in a man who would so use his own wife and daughter."

"He is a man without honor," agreed Bron.

As Eithne overheard them speak of her father, she felt shame. What little pride she had came from her mother's lineage of Myr, yet no gift was as coveted as the singer's voice and this came from her father. He had not always been without honor.

She watched Bron lovingly. Something the sea king had said caused him to shake back his long dark hair and laugh. Over his muscled shoulders his sky blue cape rippled in the breeze. More than anything in the world she wanted Bron mac Llyr to sire her daughters. He was a man with honor.

The sun was setting in a crimson death across the waves of the western sea. Astride Samisen, Eithne gazed over the low hills of Tir nan Og and watched the three swans take flight, their large wings ruffling the waters of the pond. They circled above her head and drifted like clouds toward the barrow mound.

"They are beautiful in form and flight," said Bron, who sat behind Eithne on the horse. "I envy you, Eithne. I wish I were of a kith that could fly."

Eithne smiled and said, "And I wish I were of yours. Isn't that the way of things."

"Aye, 'tis," Bron agreed.

"As a child, I was very homely, graceless, and clumsy. My hair was mousy, my neck skinny, and my eyes too big for my face. My mother assured me it would not always be so. She told me that it was the way of swan maidens to be awkward and unattractive until their thirteenth year."

"By the look of you now, she was right," he said.

"Beway, that was the distress, she wasn't. My thirteenth year came and passed and I was still as Gibbers said, 'the ugly gurrul.' In my disappointment, without my mother about to soften me in womanly ways, I became quite the wild thing. But in my sixteenth year the transformation began to take place. Each morning I'd wake and something different had changed in my face or form. And then one night, the wildness called me and I stood on the ledge of my window and leaped. For the first time I flew."

"It must have been very thrilling . . . and frightening," said Bron, guiding Samisen around a quagmire and closer to the barrow mound.

"No more than this very moment," confessed Eithne of her approaching ordeal.

Bron bent his head over her shoulder and kissed her cheek. "I have faith that you will fly through this as well."

Her love-desire for him swelled in her heart, but it could not push away her nervousness.

The clansmen awaited them at the barrow mound. Now as she and Bron approached, the men stood in a ring around a fire at the mouth of the mound. The sun was sinking behind the tumbled stones, touching them with scarlet and gold—it appeared like spilled blood.

Bron let loose her waist and slipped down onto the ground. Eithne shivered, as the rising wind tugged at her cloak. Bron had told her very little about the ordeal other than it was not common for a woman to undertake such an initiation. She was thankful for Niamh's presence at the sea king's side.

Bron turned to her, his face grave with solemnity. She put her hands on his shoulders and he helped her off Samisen. She wanted to put her arms around him and hold him, like a child afraid to leave the protection of its parent. But she knew that would be a poor showing in front of his unsmiling and somber clansmen.

Once she entered the circle, the sea king stepped forward. In his hand he held a shell drinking horn. Steam writhed above it like spindrift.

"Drink, milady, we now begin the ancient ritual of trial."

Bron had left her side and stepped into the ranks of his clansmen. Eithne looked over to him, but his eyes were shadowed. Uncertainty gripped her. She did not want to do this.

"Milady," came the sea king's quiet voice calling for her attention.

Her hands reached for the proffered shell and she lifted it to her lips. The drink tasted scalding hot and bitter as wormwood. Her throat burned, and as the stuff settled into her stomach she wondered if she was going to spew it up again. The fire gave way to numbness, and a warmth in her belly gradually spread through her until the ends of her fingers tingled.

Locking arms over shoulders, the clansmen began a low deep-voiced chanting in the oldest of tongues. The sound of their voices weighted the air with spell speaking and magic.

Then Niamh stepped before Eithne looking not the young maid but the seeress. In the wind, the strands of her black hair waved over her penetrating eyes.

"Take off your clothing, Eithne." She held a clay pot of ashes in her hands.

A quiver went through Eithne's belly, but she knew she must. First she slipped off her boots, then the cape. Awkwardly, her fingers unfastened the tangle of her shoulder ties and her tunic fell in a soft pool at her feet. Eyes lowered, the clansmen began moving counterclockwise in a slow rhythmic step around her. Briskly, Niamh rubbed the ash over Eithne's shoulders, back, and stomach, down her legs, and lastly upon her forehead and cheeks.

The men broke the circle and snaked in a curve

toward the mound's entrance. Niamh took Eithne's hand and led her behind the men. She chanted,

Out of day, comes the night—
Through the smoke of firelight—

Around them the night was growing, dimming the difference between light and shadow. Tension tightened Eithne's shoulders as she approached the gaping, black-mouthed opening of the mound. She was afraid of what was going to happen to her but, at the same time, she felt the gaze of Bron upon her, looked up, and caught a glint of reassurance in his emerald eyes.

Then she felt the push of strong hands and she stumbled into the darkness of the mound, the doorway into night. Trying to see, she turned and heard the grind of the great stone slab being rolled over the entrance, imprisoning her until the morn.

A sudden, all was cold and still.

She crouched down, silence pulsing palpably in her ears. In all that dark emptiness nothing stirred. She had to remind herself to breathe.

Bron's words returned to her: *'Tis a rare man of the isles who would not prefer to die on the open sea rather than enter a barrow mound.* Aye, she thought, the place is full of bones and death. She smelled it.

And it was full of something more. . . . She heard it moving now . . . slithering toward her. Her heart pace quickened. Her greatest imagined fears leaped into her mind's eye.

In reaction she opened her mouth to cry out, but then some sense stopped her. She shifted and moved to put her shoulders against the stone wall. After a moment of feeling here and there, she realized nothing solid was near. She felt wildly exposed. On hands and knees she crawled on the earthen floor away from the slithering sounds into deeper darkness.

When her knees began to hurt, she stopped. *You are crawling in circles,* came the small voice of reason. *Stay put.* She curled into a fetal ball and thought she might sleep, but she dared not close her eyes. Even in the pitch blackness she was afraid that if she closed her eyes and let her guard down something fearful would happen. Whatever shared the darkness with her, waited . . . and if she closed her eyes it would come.

Like a bowstring, time stretched taut, released, and stretched again. Odd sensations prickled her body and sometimes it seemed as if she had no body at all. Cradling herself against earth's bones she rocked and rocked toward sunrise.

After a while her eyelids felt like lead. They burned and watered. She fought to keep them open as fear gripped her.

And then it happened . . . her eyes fell shut and in that split second the darkness transformed . . . the evil broke loose. She blinked and saw swirling figures in the patches of darkness. The demons of her father's Unseelie Court surrounded her. She screamed, scrambled to her feet, and began running blindly.

Suddenly, her legs sank into oozing mud. She lurched, her arms flailing for handholds, then she fell. She smelled the rich tang of peat and bog as she struggled. Already she was mired to the belly, and every movement only worked her deeper in.

If I keep struggling the bog will swallow me, came her realization in snapping clarity.

Who would help her? Rising in the darkness surrounding her, the grotesque faces of her father's demons lurked. Fanged jaws hung in gaping anticipation and bulging eyes burned with a devouring fire.

Closest hovered the Fir Darrig, blood spouting from his handless arms. "Take my hand, milady," he screeched over and over.

Revulsion consumed her, and no matter if she sank all the way to hell she would never take his offered help.

And then beside her in the bog the green head of Gibbers emerged. "Like us yer evil. We're yer kith, you wicked gurrul. We're yer kith. Yer same as us," he cried foully, until Eithne covered her ears.

"You are not my kith!" she shouted at his grimacing face. "I am nothing like you. You have no souls. I have a soul."

"Are you so sure, Eithne?" Sheelin's voice was smooth as a glassy sea. She turned and saw her father just beyond her reach. White fear gripped her and she felt as if her heart had ceased to beat. Of all the visages his was the most frightening. He stood in all his black grandeur. Panic-stricken, she struggled. The movement cost her as the dank rottenness imprisoned her to below her arms. He knelt and leaned to her. "Are you so sure we have no souls?"

"Aye, you cannot love. Only those with souls love."

He took his time before speaking and when he did his tone was hauntingly mild. "And do you love, Eithne?"

"Beway! You mock me," she spat vehemently.

Unruffled, his perfect mouth curved into a smile that quit before reaching his eyes. "I merely asked you a question, my daughter."

"I wish to the moon I was not your daughter. I'm shamed by you."

"Take my hand, Eithne, and save yourself before you sink and disappear into the bog of your own shame." She glared at his proffered hand with hostility.

"I hate you," she cried out. "I hate what you've done to my mother. I hate that you will invade Myr with your dark powers. I'd rather die than take your hand. I'd rather die than be like you."

"But you are . . . like me."

"Nay, nay!" she denied, sobbing uncontrollably.

"Aye, Eithne, like me you have the singer's voice, like me you weave the powers of dark and light, like me you can breed evil." His eyes held a demonic light as he stretched out his arms to her. "Embrace me, Eithne. Together we will invade Myr. Embrace your own darkness."

Then Sheelin was gone. And before her stood herself, the self that embodied her own evil. The same demonic light reflected in her eyes. Appalled, she turned away.

Bron's words echoed in her mind like thunder: *You cannot truly love until you learn to love yourself.* She knew now what he meant. She must learn to love all facets of herself. The good and the bad. But how?

Slowly, she looked back. From behind, she heard Gibbers muttering, "Ye are more than ye think ye are."

Take my hand, said the aspect of herself she disowned. Tremors shook her body as the mire covered her shoulders.

Feeling utterly wretched, she dug her fingers into the slime and dragged herself toward the other Eithne. Her limbs moved with lethargy and she wondered if she might ever free herself. Then she was staggering forward on solid ground. Her breast heaving, she clasped the proffered hand. Racked with sobs, she collapsed to her knees. Despite her loathing, she embraced her own darkness.

Beway, beway, comforted the dark aspect of herself. *You are evil as well as good.*

And Eithne knew that was more truth than she herself had wanted to accept until then. She felt the light touch of a hand upon her hair.

You are worthy of love as you are. I love you.

She felt the other Eithne's arms tighten around her. In that moment she felt freer than flight and light engulfed her like the noonday sun. Her crying slowed and her tears became tears of joy. Peace filled her and she sank into a sleep that was as restoring and healing as any fairy enchantment.

"Eithne, my love. 'Tis over. We're here now." It was Bron's voice she heard as the clansmen rolled away the great stone blocking the entrance to the mound. She was coiled on the ground, her arms hugging herself. She blinked, unable to decipher the faces. Strong hands lifted her.

They carried her out into the morning sunrise. She realized that the ordeal was over. As her eyes adjusted, everything became clearer, brighter, and more vibrant. The sea crashed against the cliffs and the gulls cried in an awakening din. She was alive.

She sought out Bron's face. It was lined from sleeplessness. He appeared as if he'd traversed his own night of fear. She offered him a timid, heartfelt smile. He stepped forward and embraced her a long, long reviving moment.

Then he whispered softly in her ear. "It's not a matter of slaying your dragons, Eithne, love. It's a matter of embracing them."

He drew back.

Niamh came up and blessed her with alder, willow, and oak, and hung a wreath of sea flowers around her neck. Then, Bron lifted her upon Samisen. They rode down to the sea and by his own hand he bathed her. She reveled in his touch and his careful washing away of the black ash. The water was cold, but it invigorated her with the vitality of life itself. She found her voice and began singing out to sea. Her voice was higher and purer and her song more lilting and joyous than ever before. Encircling her on the beach, the others came to hear her song.

When she ceased, the sea king stood by her. His face kindly, he said, "You have survived the night of fear. You've had the courage to face the enemy within. You are now of our clan, milady Eithne. By my word we adopt you into our sea clan."

He removed his sky blue cloak and placed it over her bare shoulders. Tears welled in her eyes and she drew it around her with pride.

The clansmen lifted their swords. The blades gleamed in the sunlight. Together in bold salute they shouted, "Arrah! Arrah!"

Bron stood beside her. His gaze was an endearment. He said loudly, "You are well-loved, my Lady Eithne."

She smiled and declared proudly, "And I now love myself as well, Bron mac Llyr."

Bron left Eithne in the croft napping through the afternoon and wandered along the shore. Long strands of seaweed splayed like grasping fingers over the barnacle faced rocks. The waves shattered against the cliffs in the persistent heartbeat of the sea. The foaming white water ran hissing up the beach almost to his bare feet as he made his way along.

As he walked onto a sandy spit, a flash of silver caught his eye. He stopped and squinted into the shining mirror of the sea. There was a shimmering silver shape moving through the water toward him.

He grinned widely and rested his hand upon his hip. He watched and waited. Aye, he thought. 'Tis Sarenn come a snooping.

Soon she rose from the sea and the waves lifted her onto the land. She stretched languorously, running her fingers through her mane of long golden hair that glittered with sea diamonds. She was as slim hipped and high-breasted as the first time he had seen her rising from the sea.

"Hallo, Bron mac Llyr," she said, flirtatiously.

"Hallo back, Sarenn."

He watched her unclasp her water cloak and spread it upon the beach. She arched her back and reached her hands skyward as if exulting in the caress of the wind on her naked body.

"Will you not come and sit beside me?" she bid enticingly.

"If you give me your promise not to pull me into the sea."

"You have it." Her smile was elfin.

He sat down next to her on her cloak. She coiled up on her long tail, leaned toward him, and kissed him fully on the mouth. The taste of fish lingered on his lips after she drew away.

There was a time when her single kiss could ignite his youthful passion. But no more. She was a past flame not to be rekindled.

"You're still partial to herring," he said, running his tongue over his lower lip.

"I am." She bestowed upon him a coquettish eye. "And you seem to be partial to swan."

He chuckled. "I am that. I'll admit it. She told me she met you in the sea cave."

Sarenn frowned. "I did not like her."

Bron tried not to smile. Sarenn rarely liked anyone who did not succumb to her charms. "And why not?" he asked with mock innocence.

Her voice was cool. "I do not like her because you love her."

Bron laughed outright. He enjoyed Sarenn and knew that sea maidens held no notion of time. As far as Sarenn was concerned their affair was as fresh as today's mackerel catch.

"I know you are not still pining for me. You are notoriously fickle," he observed.

She shrugged a delicate shoulder. "True. Had not your father come, I was soon to cast you out of my domain anyway."

"Then . . . " he said slowly. "It is I who was spurned by you."

Her hot bluebell eyes flashed. "That is right!"

Suddenly, he clutched his heart dramatically. "Och, you wound me to the very core."

"I'm sure you'll mend," she said with a lack of sincerity. "And if you are to tell it about, have the grace to tell it true."

And now he understood the reason for her visit. She was here to save face. Her reputation as a seductress might be sullied if it was found out that one of her paramours was free enough of her enchantments to fall in love with another woman.

"Aye." He grinned. "I'll tell it true."

"Good. It is settled between us. Now," she said, taking up the end of her water cloak, "I'm off."

He came to his feet. She moved down the beach and stood by the edge of the waves, the long silver-shot sea cloak fluttering about her bare shoulders. He admired her otherworldly beauty. She turned her head slowly, a ghost of a smile playing about her lips, then she leaped into the waves.

Chapter
15

Night crept slowly over Tir nan Og. The tiny sliver of the moon touched the billowing plumes of clouds in the black cauldron sky. Eithne and Bron stood outside the croft and watched the campfires of their clansmen shine on the outer limits of the circle of stones like fairy lights.

Bron encircled Eithne's shoulders with one arm. "'Tis so calm tonight. Nary a breeze blows from the sea. Niamh believes that 'tis a sign that Sheelin is not far away."

Eithne nestled close to Bron and sighed. "I no longer fear him. Let him come."

They stood awhile longer, staring silently into the night, content in each other's company.

Suddenly, Eithne shivered.

"Are you cold?" asked Bron. He pulled her cloak more tightly about her.

"A wee bit. Let us go inside," she said.

"Aye, the day has been full."

"That it has," she said, still shivering.

She entered the croft and reached for the teapot. Her hand trembled and she made sloppy work of pouring a cupful.

"Let me," said Bron, his face gaunt with deep lines of concern. By the time she drank the cup, she was shaking so badly she could hardly stand. Bron placed his hand on her brow, but she was not feverish. Lifting her in his strong arms, he carried her to the bed and wrapped the thick furs about her.

She saw the circumspect glance that passed between Bron and Niamh. They both knew as she did that Sheelin was drawing upon her essence.

"Stay near," she requested to Bron.

"Are you afraid?" he asked as he lay down beside her, curving his own body next to her own.

"Nay, I'm not. But he weakens me. 'Tis as if he knows I am stronger now."

"Try to sleep," encouraged Bron, trailing a kiss across her cheek.

Eithne was not so content with just a kiss. She sought out his lips and pressed her own to them, sweetly probing. He responded fervently. Desire for him rose in Eithne, but the straight back of Niamh silhouetted before the fire thwarted that need. Even so, as she drew away his mouth returned to hers insistent and urgent. His hands slipped beneath the furs and cupped her buttocks and pulled them to him with a firm pressure. The cloth that separated her wantonness from his could not impede the tingling flow of desire that caused her to move instinctively against him.

In the next moments, their mutual passion was

inflamed in the exploration of tongue and lips. Eithne tried ever so hard not to breathe too loudly or whimper the sighing moans of her coursing heart.

It was Niamh's overobvious clearing of her throat that caused them to break apart. "I believe I'll take the night air," she announced, coming to her feet. She snatched up her cloak and walked to the door.

Bron opened his mouth to speak, but Eithne hastily placed her fingers over his lips and whispered, "Let her go. We've had no time together since they've come." Then her voice more intense, she murmured, "I need you."

The door had barely creaked shut than Bron and Eithne were skin to skin and heart to heart beneath the mound of blankets and furs. It seemed a hundred years had passed since such intimacy between them.

The foreboding of what might come in the next days added a desperation to their loving. She blessed the touch of his sole hand upon her, the soft stroking that splayed over each thigh in turn and moved in soft swirls across her belly, up between her breasts and then first to one breast, then the other, cupping, and then fastening lightly on one nipple that sent a jolt of pure sensation through her.

His dark head bent and she felt his lips upon her breasts, first teasing, then sucking more strongly until the nipples had grown hard and tingling. Then he abandoned them, easing her thighs farther apart. Her hands tangled in his thick hair. He lifted his head and gazed into her eyes soulfully.

"Do you want me?"

"Beway," she rasped. "Does the sea dance on the shores of Tir nan Og?"

He lifted himself above her, and she waited in aching emptiness for the hard swell of his manhood to fill her. He covered her then, skin touching skin. She opened to him and her hips lifted as she felt the delicious pressure enter her. She could feel his heart coursing against her own. His whole weight came down upon her and they began the slow, pulsing, winging dance of spirit and heart entwined. The impassioned rush of his vitality infused her, revived and restored her own weakened state. Transforming to swan spirit, she drank from his essence the golden elixir of ecstasy.

At first light, Eithne awoke. The room was like a great long fire. Scrambling from the smothering blankets, she went and opened the door. Not even a breeze trickled through. She felt suffocated and her light shift weighed upon her like a warrior's mail.

"What is it?" Bron came to his feet and pulled on his leggings and tunic.

"There is no air. I cannot breathe." She stepped outside. "Quickly, Bron," she called. "Look." She pointed to a great ship off the headland of the northern shore. "Its sails billow, yet there is no wind."

"Aye, Sheelin's come and all with him is sorcery and illusion." He took her in his arms and cautioned, "Remember, you must love more than fear."

She studied his emerald eyes. "How can I not love when I am loved by one such as you?" Then she smiled and pulled away a swan feather entangled in his hair. "You must keep this for good luck and as a sign that we'll never be parted in spirit." She stood on her tiptoes and tied it securely onto his long braided hair swatch. "Hurry now, I'll wake Niamh."

Reluctantly, he drew away and left her. He disappeared around the corner to the stable. Eithne ran inside the croft and nudged Niamh awake on her pallet. "Sheelin's come. We must seek safe haven with our clansmen in the circle of stones."

"I dreamed it!" Niamh was up dressing and was soon outside before Eithne. In the door yard, Bron lifted her and then Eithne upon Samisen. He climbed on himself and prodded Samisen into a brisk gallop.

"Arrah!" Niamh gestured skyward. "The scald-crow flies."

Eithne saw the gruesome winged harpy with trailing hair and talons flying over the stone henge.

"She presages death and defeat—"

"Shush! Niamh," interrupted Bron, sharply. "You've no need to carp on so. . . ."

Eithne clasped Niamh's hand comfortingly and said, "'Tis illusion, Niamh. The great ship, the warriors, the scald-crow . . . 'tis illusion."

By the time the three arrived at the stone henge, the ship had dropped sail.

"Both of you, take refuge within the protection of the stones," commanded Bron as he lifted each one down.

Eithne stepped past the sea clansmen who stood shoulder to shoulder on the outer edge of the stone henge, their swords raised in preparedness.

"We will make our stand here, as agreed," said the sea king to Bron. "You were right, the Fomorians are with him. Close behind comes another ship."

Eithne saw the second ship moving into the inlet. She stiffened, as she watched Sheelin's Unseelie Court pour over the ship's sides and into the surf. But what held her eye was the figure of Sheelin himself riding a black war-horse up the beach. He rode in lead like a fierce warlord. His midnight cloak was thrown back and light reflected off his bronzed winged battle helmet. He looked the stuff of legend and nightmare.

She clutched Bron's arm, drawing reassurance from his solid warmth. "Listen," she whispered.

"I hear nothing . . ." he said after a moment.

And then Niamh said, "I hear it."

"Singing. 'Tis ever so soft," said Eithne.

Then a sudden, a flock of white swans came winging down and landed all around them. Shedding their swan plumage, they transformed into the fairest of women. Before Eithne stood Ketha. She fell into her mother's arms and held her close.

"Oh, Mother. You've come," breathed Eithne.

"The sea king summoned us," said Ketha, her own visage almost a mirror of her daughter's. She seemed fragile and slender beneath the feathered cape draped over her shoulders.

"But how?" asked Eithne.

"On the ley path . . . the stone circles here as well as at Rath Morna paths between the two worlds."

"Is that what you meant when you told me that there was another world hidden in this one?"

"Aye."

"And is that how Sheelin intends to enter Myr?" asked Eithne.

"Unless he has the power of the singer's voice, he cannot. Even now he draws from you that essence."

A horn sounded. Ketha turned, her eyes riveting to the dark form of Sheelin upon the cliff top. Eithne stared as well.

The sea king was riding toward him on Samisen. Sheelin's stallion moved skittishly, its metal shod hooves ringing hollowly against the cliff face.

"I never knew it would come to this." Ketha sighed.

"'Tis not your doing," soothed Bron, his own gaze hard on the parlance.

Eithne watched the sea king rein Samisen to a halt before Sheelin. "Identify yourself," he called, his voice stern and knowing.

"I am Sheelin of Rath Morna. I come for my daughter, Eithne." His face was impassive as if carved from stone.

"'Tis my understanding that Eithne has no wish to go with you," said the sea king, smiling thinly.

"You cannot refuse me!" His features held fleetingly the telltale sign of his consternation. "You are inviting your death and that of your clansmen. Do you not know that?"

"Arrah! That is your speaking not mine," retaliated the sea king.

"Then it begins," shouted Sheelin, his eyes flashing and the fire of anger flushing his cheeks. "She is my daughter and I will take her!"

The sea king turned Samisen about and the horse fairly flew back to the henge. Eithne glanced at Bron's face. She shivered at the brooding fire in his green eyes as he watched the approaching warriors of Sheelin's Unseelie Court. How fierce they appeared with horn and drum sounding. Their broad shoulder armor flashed silver and their swords and spears pointed to the gray skies.

Heads together in conversation, Ketha was beside the sea king. Eithne overheard his words, "A little magic . . ." And Eithne wondered who would pay the price for "a little magic" this day.

Beside her, Bron joined with his clansmen in deep-voiced chanting. Suddenly, all fell silent. Then, around her everyone disappeared. She scanned the outer circle of the henge and saw only the halting and confused warriors of Sheelin's court. Was she left alone to face them?

"Bron? Niamh?" cried Eithne.

"I am here, Eithne," came Bron's voice. "They do not see us. We are under the spell of *faet fiada* . . . the cloak of invisibility."

And again the sea clansmen broke into spell chanting that exposed the illusion of Sheelin's army. Their true forms—trolls, dwarfs, shellycoats, and all manner of beasties—were revealed.

And then above, the skies filled with dark forms. Eithne heard the rustling of wings. She lifted her eyes to see taloned and vicious beaked raptors descending upon Sheelin's menagerie. What a howling and shrieking came forth as the wretches slithered and crawled in all directions seeking safe haven.

It was a pathetic sight. Sheelin flung curses and oaths at their heads while most dispersed into the nearby bogs and cliff holes. His own black steed transformed into a young kelpie that bucked him off and he was left afoot.

But his defeat was short-lived, as the sea clansmen's cloak of invisibility weakened. Threateningly, the battle cries of the approaching Fomorians and the baying of their war hounds echoed off cliff and sea.

"That is no illusion," whispered Niamh returning to visibility at Eithne's side.

Around Eithne all the sea clansmen took form. She saw Bron standing with his clansmen, a spear in his hand. But where was her mother? She saw none of the swan sisters. Then she looked upward and saw the raptors still circling above like the scald-crow awaiting death. Aye, she thought again, more and more magic . . . who will pay?

And then more frightening than imagination, the Fomorians appeared on the hillside. As Bron had told her the Fomorians were a grotesque race whose origins were in the chaotic times of old earth. Some were hairless and simian. Some had men's bodies and the sleek heads of horses. Others had doleful human faces, peering from bullet heads. They rattled their scabbards and dashed their spears against their shields making a thunderous outcry.

Dread filled Eithne as their iron shod war hounds ran in front, the unmistakable howling of bloodlust in their cries. They were gigantic beasts, standing almost fifteen hands high. Their eyes were wild and burned with a demonic intelligence.

One beast pulled ahead of the others and, though it was almost twenty paces away, it leaped for a clansman's throat. Bron threw himself to the hard ground and tilted the point of his spear upward. The huge dog came down onto the spear point, its great jaws snapping the shaft. It coughed and choked; blood slavered over Bron's tunic. The heavy carcass fell on him, pinning him to the ground. A clansman stepped forward and hefted the dead hound off him only to turn and face another.

And then Eithne stared aghast as something strange and terrifying happened. The war hound that Bron had slain struggled back to its feet and once more attacked. And again with single hand Bron slew it . . . and minutes later again it clambered to its feet.

Beway, thought Eithne. *'Tis the darkest of sorcery.* All around she watched as one Fomorian after another was slain and then rose up again, to join the living dead.

She scanned the battleground. Where was Sheelin? Because of his sorcery her clansmen were dying. It must be stopped.

"Eithne!" she heard Bron's voice calling to her. "You must sing!" Even as he spoke, she began running to a center stone and, reaching for hand- and footholds, she climbed onto the flat slab of the capstone.

In full view of all she began singing, falteringly at first because she'd not her full strength of voice. Against the clamor of shield and clash of swords, she composed a song of ancient knowledge from deep within her very essence to transform the chaos. It was a song that showed she possessed a sorceress's understanding of the workings of enchantments.

Easily, she called forth lightning and thunder,

which distracted the war hounds and set them baying and howling for cover. The winds rose and the east grew dark with storm clouds.

Then Sheelin was facing her, just outside the circle. He sat astride a triple-headed Chimera that reared, breathing fire and lashing out with its claws. His bold face was fine-drawn and seemed to flicker, betraying an unfathomable emotion. It was not love, she could be sure. . . .

Unflinching, she continued singing, her voice now strong and clear. As she sang, the Fomorians' swords exploded with the flash of lightning and their spears turned into frail reeds. Shooting through the storm-filled skies, their arrows sprouted wings and landed in the sea. Their battle armor flew off piece by piece, landing in the boggy earth.

Eithne sang on and on, in verse as old as earth's very heart. The Fomorians were routed, and as they retreated, their feet became like heavy stones that left them writhing in place as harmless as slugs.

But still before her remained one who was not so harmless . . . Sheelin. His face was no longer impassive and his black eyes penetrated her like dragon's breath in the night. His unspoken threat rolled in the sea air, as thick and searing as molten fire over flesh.

His hand went beneath his black cloak and slowly he retrieved a large, crystal orb. Eithne's heart plunged. What sorcery would he work now she could not know.

Above her the raptors began transforming into white swans against the blackened skies. They circled around her head as if casting a magical ring. She sang louder, intensely, the cords stood out on her neck with urgency.

Sheelin lifted his hand aloft, and in a thundering voice he cried out an oath of spell speaking and threw the crystal orb to the ground. It shattered in a burst of glistening shards.

The air trembled and vibrated as the destructive elements were unleashed. Thunder and lightning continued to detonate all about, engulfing them with flashing light and earsplitting sound. Icy blasts of wind whipped in from the turbulent sea and driving rain pelted Eithne's face.

And then the earth began to move and split apart. The great stones shuddered and toppled.

Eithne knew he'd broken the seal between the two worlds. Her voice began to weaken. Her throat ached. How easy it would be to stop, to let herself sink into the rising darkness and be consumed. But the survival of Myr was more precious than her own life and she had no choice but to sing on.

She sang, a brilliant keening, conjuring a mending for the rending between the worlds. Once again the earth shook mightily, a final tremor . . . Sheelin was finished. The last of his illusions, the three-headed Chimera, vanished in the face of Eithne's singing. She collapsed and fell from the capstone.

Bron caught the limp and white-faced Eithne in his arms. "Eithne!" he cried, looking down at her, his own heart breaking. "This day you pay the price of magic, my love."

Her eyelids lifted and almost inaudibly she whispered, "Aye . . . and happily. My father . . . take me to my father."

Bron's gaze focused on Sheelin, still held outside the stone henge by the power of Eithne's song. Cradling her in his arms, Bron crossed over to Sheelin, who stood stunned amid the fallen stones and the ruins of his army.

Even to Bron his granite face was frightening in its emptiness of soul. But Eithne, her eyes brilliant with the light of passing, reached out to him. Sheelin hesitated before he took her hand in his own.

"I love you, Father," she voiced softly.

Not even Sheelin could misread the wealth of love in her manner. A nimbus of light shone all around her and she radiated more beauty than the morning star or the winter moon. In those seconds, Bron witnessed a miraculous dawning. Sheelin's cold features softened, his eyes shifted from dark to light and a single tear rolled down his cheek. Eithne's love had somehow revived that last spark of spirit in him.

Her gaze shifted to Bron and her mouth moved but he could barely hear. He bent his head and turned his ear to her lips. Her farewell words and breath became a binding caress.

Slowly she spoke forming each word with exceeding effort. "Deep peace on the running wave to you. Deep peace on the flowing air to you. Deep peace in the shining stars to you. Deep peace on the gentle night to you. Moon and stars pour their healing light on you.

Deep peace to you, Bron mac Llyr." Her words faded . . . with her breath.

Holding her, he fell to his knees and clutched her against him. He pressed his lips against her hair. "Beway, my beloved," the words whispered through him. "Your love sets you free. . . ."

Chapter
16

A dark fog crept over Tir nan Og. It was such a fog as had never been seen before in the Isles of the Blest. It was filled with the weeping of gentle voices and the phantom visages of sorrowing faces.

In deep mourning, Bron had carried Eithne's body to the croft. There he laid her down on the bed and retreated to the hearth as Ketha and Niamh prepared her body. He watched them begin to remove her clothes and bathe her naked body with springwater. Reluctantly, he turned his gaze to Sheelin, who stood at the foot of the bed. He was a broken man. His shoulders were stooped and his head hung like a dazed and abandoned child. Bron agonized . . . what a price to pay for power, yet he could not hate Sheelin.

Bron watched Ketha's delicate hands . . . so like Eithne's own . . . as she pressed the water-soaked cloth to Eithne's lifeless brow . . . her cheeks . . . her lips, lips he longed to kiss back to life. Her ministerings moved, over oval breasts and lower to the hollow of her belly and across each long slim leg.

The two women prepared her lovingly. They lifted her limp arms and slipped a fine homespun dress over her white shoulders. When Niamh cocooned her in the sky blue cloak of the sea clan, moisture welled in Bron's eyes to remember the joy she had expressed at being accepted in his clan.

With a seashell comb, Ketha attempted to tame the wild strands of Eithne's hair. Bron stepped forward. Carefully, he raked his fingers through the wild mass, smoothing it over the pillow like a flaming halo. She sleeps the dreamless sleep, he thought.

In all the tangled skein of his life the one bright thread was his love for Eithne and hers for him. He felt a gaping emptiness. Hurting more than if he'd been ripped to bits by a hundred Fomorian war hounds, he bent low and kissed her lips. He walked to the corner and picked up his harp and then strode out of the croft.

Through the thickening veil of fog, he heard his father shout the orders to light the balefires to show the spirits of the battle dead the way home. Now and again as the fog shifted he glimpsed the stabbing flames against the shroud of the bleak landscape. He sighed and breathed in the acrid scent of smoke from the balefires. As he walked, foremost in his mind was but one task. He alone would build Eithne's funeral pyre. He would ignite the pyre with the kindling of his own harp.

All night long, pausing not for drink or sleep, he single-handedly toiled. Some of his clansmen approached and offered their assistance, but he refused as was his by right. Driven by grief, he climbed and stumbled up the cliffs, carrying the sea washed stones and driftwood from the fog shrouded beaches to the center of the henge. He filled the spaces between the stones with soft, velvety moss and carefully wove and crisscrossed the salt soaked wood around the stone altar.

The fog did not lift with the first light of dawn. Chilled, and with a suffocating ache in his heart, Bron examined his handiwork. Then, lastly, he placed his harp at the foot of the pyre. Here his beloved would begin the journey on the road of the dead. He stared at the stump of his sword hand. He cursed his lot that he was unable to play his harp and the ancient coronach of his clan for her passing. Yet, in spirit the harp would accompany her on the journey.

Aye, he thought, all of him wished to embark on the journey with her as well. That was the pain. Even now, he could not raise his gaze and not hope that she would walk out of the mists, smiling and alive. He grew still, listening to the sea and from the sound he knew the tide was turning. Feeling beaten and in all-encompassing despair, he cast himself onto the ground and let loose his grief.

The croft was still with death. Ketha kept wake over Eithne's body. She watched the flames of the fire as she waited for Niamh to return with the sea clansmen. Sheelin sat in the corner against the cold stone wall of the croft. He seemed asleep. The part of her that ever had loved him longed to give him comfort, but she sensed he was comfortless.

Quietly, Ketha rose, padded over, and touched him gently on the shoulder with her hand. His eyes flickered open and for a moment he stared up at her.

"What do you want? Am I not tormented enough?" he muttered.

"I want nothing from you, Sheelin," said Ketha, kneeling before him. "I share in your sorrow."

"How can you? You were not responsible for her death. Because of me Eithne is dead. Go away from me. I cannot bear your accusing eyes upon me."

"I do not accuse you. You accuse yourself."

"Leave me be." He turned his face away from her.

"I'll not leave you be. How will love ever enter your heart? It is like a lump of cold clay. If you keep yourself apart from others, I see no hope for you. Look at me, Sheelin," she pleaded. "Look at me and know I love you."

Still refusing to meet her gaze, Sheelin groaned wretchedly. "I do not deserve your or anyone's love."

"Maybe not," Ketha agreed. "But you do deserve to love . . . loving is the greater gift. Can you love me?"

Sheelin buried his head in his hands and began to weep. Ketha reached for him. Like a drowning man, his arms caught hold of her. In his desperation, he held her close and she felt the trembling of his grief stricken body. Aye, she thought, he would suffer until the end of his days for his deeds.

Suddenly, he started to gasp for breath and rasped, "My chest feels as if a great weight is pressing against it." He fell back and his hands clutched his breast. "Aaahh . . ." he cried out. "I cannot stand the pain."

Ketha was beside him, laying her own hands over his. "Your heart is breaking open, Sheelin. Do not resist. Open your heart to love . . . or you will die."

He let loose an anguished, soul-shaking cry that reverberated off the stone walls and beyond.

"Let go," cried Ketha. "Surrender . . . to love. . . ."

She cradled him in her arms, seeing the tears streaming down his cheeks like the bursting of spring torrents down a mountainside. His body shook with the force of deep wrenching sobs. As she gazed into his eyes, she saw in their depths that last spark of his spirit reviving. She knew that raindrops could wear a hollow in the hardest stone, and that the waves of the sea could smooth the most jagged rocks. The stone of Sheelin's heart had cracked asunder and like a seed breaks forth from the dark earth to bloom, she witnessed the miracle of his reawakening love. Within his embrace she felt the warmth of his awakened heart radiate against her breast.

He wept for a long time. Then he wiped his cheeks and soulfully gazed at Ketha. Softly, he began to speak. "It feels as if I've been sleeping in a long nightmare. I've been walking down an endless black tunnel and now for the first time in a long while I see light. Where I have been, I do not wish to go again." His voice fell silent as he fell into the reverie of his thoughts.

Then he kissed Ketha's forehead, and then her lips. "I love you, Ketha," he breathed with heartfelt sincerity.

It was Ketha, who now began to weep, not from sorrow, but joy. The old Sheelin had returned.

It might have been hours, or only minutes, when Bron again lifted his head. The shroud of fog still hung over Tir nan Og. Nearby, he heard the most pitiful of blubbering. Sniffing the air, he caught the scent of troll. He came to his feet and walked around the stone pyre. There he discovered the miserable form of Gibbers. Anger seized him. Gibbers's presence seemed to defile the hallowedness of the surrounding circle.

Bron reached out and grabbed him by the neck, picked him up, and dangled him before his face. "I told you, I never wanted to see you again!"

"Och! Sure, ye don't mane it, ye cudn't be so cruel," he gargled, his eyes pleading. "Isss it true ssshe is dead?"

"Aye!" Bron glared at him, controlling the urge to take out his own frustrations on Gibbers.

Gibbers's mouth cracked wide. He broke into new heights of mournful yowling.

Then suddenly, Bron's own mouth fell open with awe. He held Gibbers's neck with his sword hand . . . fingers and all.

It was no illusion. He had feeling and strength. He let go of Gibbers's neck. Whimpering, Gibbers thudded to the ground and scrambled away to hide behind a toppled stone.

Bron paid no heed. His own attention was upon the miracle of his hand. Slowly, he flexed his fingers open and shut. There was feeling and strength in his hand.

No scar marked his wrist to show his hand had ever been severed. How? And after all this time? It was not magic, but miracle . . . love's miracle. He could not doubt that it was Eithne's final gift to him.

The sound of a single drum heralded the approaching of the procession of his clansmen. He lifted his gaze from his hand and saw the glow of torchlight through the fog. On a pallet of woven marrum grass his clansmen carried Eithne upon their shoulders.

The miracle of his restored hand paled against the starkness of her lifeless body. In this moment his hand was of small consequence. He felt guilty, wondering if Eithne's death had somehow been the ransom for not only the safety of Myr but his restored hand as well. He let his arm fall to his side and walked to meet them.

In forefront came his father with Niamh at his elbow. Behind walked Sheelin and Ketha. Bron's eyes narrowed as he scanned the face of Sheelin. He was different. Dark lines of grief were now graven in his once compassionless brow. Yet, his features seemed softened with a goodness that Bron had not perceived before.

Bron stepped into the strong embrace of his father's arms. Openly, before their clansmen they wept in shared grief. Bron remembered as a boy when his mother died. Then, he was too young to fully understand the loss a man feels for the woman he loves. In this moment, he felt every agonizing rend of the heart.

When the sea king released him there was puzzlement in his eyes. "What has happened? Your hand?"

"I do not understand it myself. But"—Bron looked over at Sheelin—"'tis no illusion."

Ketha, her beautiful face knowing, said, "The world is ever full of wonders."

Sheelin nodded with agreement. To Bron he said, "I am not the man I was. This day brings more than one miracle."

Seeing his face, Bron believed it was so. He extended his hand to Sheelin and made peace with him. Yet, like two separate tides, joy at Sheelin's change of heart and grief over Eithne's loss moved within him.

Carefully, the clansmen laid Eithne down upon the pyre. Bron stood there, very still and unspeaking, gazing on her face. Below from the sea came the endless shush and shurr of the waves against the cliffs. At his back the wind off the ocean was very cold.

Ketha stepped forward and laid her feather cloak over Eithne, and drew away. Bron first heard a sweet keening and then from the mists came winging down the swan sisters of Myr. They shook off their swan plumage and took form as women within the circle of the sea clansmen.

The sea king drew up and initiated tribute to the Lady Eithne reflecting, "The champion's light shining from you, your singer's voice enjoined upon the field of battle. At your song our foes fled."

The strong voices of the clansmen lifted in unison. "She shines for all of us, she burns within all of us."

"Sister among us," sang the women, "we thank you, bless you, and release you, and ask that your fire remain with us. The circle is open, but not unbroken."

The fog was lifting. The sea king gave the order to Drunn to pour oil over the wood before the pyre was torched.

"Wait, Father," said Bron, retrieving his harp. "I wish to play the coronach."

Acquiescing, his father signaled Drunn with a halting hand.

A brief moment of apprehension touched Bron. What if he could no longer play? He flexed his fingers and carefully plucked one string. The one single note, deep and potent, sounded over the island and rang off the granite faces of the stones as if it called a command.

"Look," shouted a clansman, pointing down to the cove below. The sleek forms of a pair of dolphins burst out of the sea, surfaced, and arched through the air with serene beauty. To the sea clansmen it was a remarkable omen, a symbol of the eternal round.

More encouraged, Bron brushed his fingers over the harp strings in a series of minor harmonies. And then into the air flowed the sweet shimmer of music, and light and color seemed to swirl around him. His music expressed the many shades of his emotion from the whirl of exaltation to the wildest lament. It seemed to some that in the bogs the reeds and rushes swayed and over the sea the winged ones soared freer. The lilt of love was in his playing and all the interlace of life that was the sweet singing of his heart.

While he played, he watched his beloved Eithne. A sudden, her pale nostrils widened, the eyelids flickered, and the curled fingers trembled. Her delicate body shuddered as if from a struggle deep within. Color returned to her cheeks. Then a great gasp of breath escaped her throat and her eyes opened. Her gaze flew like a homing dove to Bron.

For a moment the flow of force between them was almost visible for any who could see. He dropped his harp. Falling to his knees beside her, he seized her hand and pressed a kiss upon her palm.

A great "Arrah!" arose from the sea clansmen and the swan sisters proclaimed their joy in jubilant cries. And then the sun rose around them and lanced the mists with spearing golden rays. The earth greened, birds began singing, and the sea shone crystalline against a shining shore. Wildflowers carpeted the heath and their wonderful fresh fragrance filled the air.

Eithne sat up.

The sunlight danced around her so brightly that it struck her eyes like flame. She gazed lovingly into Bron's face and caressed his cheek as if she were not sure whether she dreamed.

His heart pounding, Bron clasped Eithne to his chest.

Wonderment filled her face. She gazed around, seeing her mother and then Sheelin. "Where are we?" she murmured.

"We are in Myr." Ketha smiled, waving her hand. "The love between you has reversed the laws of the two worlds. Your hearts have broken through the barriers of time, space, and death. In the simple act of your love, all has been transformed."

Though this all seemed wondrously shocking to Eithne, Bron's presence filled her with reassuring warmth. With a sideways glance she made a lover's inventory of him and discovered he'd not transformed so greatly that he had lost that touch of desire in his emerald eyes. She also hoped he'd not passed beyond taking her in his arms in wild abandonment.

Her blood quickened its sluggish course when he bent to touch his lips to her own.

"Do that again," she asked.

"What?"

"Kiss my lips. It stirs my blood and that is undeniably healthy for one who so recently has been a corpse." She held him in a hot, wanton gaze that teased.

"I want to kiss your mouth and more. I want to take you in my arms."

"Only that?" she prompted with mock innocence.

His hands took and held her own lightly. "In truth I want to carry you away to some deserted spot and make love to you," he confessed. "But I fear this is not the time."

She looked down and cried out, "You have both hands!"

"Aye." His white teeth flashed an overwhelming smile. "'Twas one of the many miracles this day."

"Beway," she breathed, her eyes large and luminous. "It was your harp music I heard. I was aboard a ship, one akin to the Wave Sweeper, setting off to the faraway isles. I heard the slap of waves against its hull, and the splash as an anchor was raising. The sails were being run up the mast and billowed as the wind filled them. But it was then I heard the harp music. My senses tingled as the notes chimed like fairy bells on the wind."

Tears glistened on her cheeks. "Oh, Bron, that music touched my heart with such deep yearning, that it was then I told the shipman, I must go back. When I opened my eyes you were there." She laid her face against his shoulder, feeling the rough texture of his tunic and inhaling the familiar aroma of his breath.

"Come," he prompted, lifting her to her feet. "Unless you wish to continue lying upon your funeral pyre. 'Tis well oiled and awaiting the torch."

"Begorrah," she jested. "My nose may be still cold, but not that cold." She nuzzled it against his hair and peeked over his shoulder. She smiled at all those around as first Ketha, then Sheelin, moved to embrace her.

She felt herself being drawn in the warm oval of her father's arms—she realized for the first time in her remembrance. His clasp was startling in its strength and tenderness. The darkness that she'd ever sensed around him had dissipated and she felt a flow of love between them. Her throat ached, not as a result of his magics, but from her desire to tell him again that she loved him.

Before she could speak, his own words erupted. "Forgive me, Eithne. I love you, my daughter."

In the soft folds of his cloak she wept softly with joy, and then reluctantly moved to embrace others.

"Do I smell troll?" A sudden, she sniffed the air and

looked about. She spied a green flash of color dash behind a fallen stone. She walked over. "You must come out, Gibbers."

The tip of his pointed ears appeared over the stone and Eithne heard his small whining voice. "I'm here, but I'm afeared."

"'Tis only me . . . the evil, wicked gurrul."

What an outburst of wailing followed. "I niver, thruly belaffed ye were an evil, wicked gurrul," he sniveled. His gob green eyes, running wet and overflowing with misery, came into view. Pointing a bony finger at Bron he declared, "That one 'ill murdher me if I show me face."

"Is that so?" asked Eithne, watching Bron with amusement in her eyes.

"'Tis no more than he deserves." Bron winked conspiratorially.

"Can you promise to speak well of all?" examined Eithne.

"Troth, nary a foul ward can pass me lips. Me hart has turned," Gibbers vowed, touching his breast.

"I think his heart turns because at his feet the heath is a mass of violets," challenged Bron. Gibbers shook his head in denial. "But if he's a particular favorite of your heart, milady . . . I'll show mercy."

"That he is!" affirmed Eithne.

Gibbers's lipless mouth spread wide with delight and he scrambled atop the stone slab in full view as if he were about to wear the crown of the hour.

There was a companionable silence that stretched for some moments, before Bron bowed gallantly and offered his arm to Eithne. "Milady, would you honor me by taking a stroll in this fair land of Myr?"

"Indeed, I will, Bron mac Llyr," agreed Eithne. She raised her head, just a little, to look into his eyes and there she saw a wealth of love and promise. He smiled in a way that made her heart expand like a moon daylight bright. With resilient eyes they held each other's gaze, entwining fingers and hands.

Soft confidences flowed between them as they strolled from the hallowed henge, his head slightly bent to catch her words, his arm around her shoulders, hers lightly encircling his narrow hips.

"Musha," beamed Gibbers on the aside to all who cared to listen. "I knew their sssecret all along. He loved her betther than life. An' she axed was it in airnest he was, an' he said cud she doubt it whin he loved her wid all the veins av his heart."

Gibbers gave a dramatic sigh as he saw the two lovers disappear over the rolling hill. Munching on a handful of violets, he prattled on, "An' now they both think the trouble is all over foriver. It's a way thim lovers has, an' they must be axcused, bekase it's the same wid thim all."

Author's Note

I would like to credit research sources I have used in writing this story: *The Enchanted World Series* published by Time-Life Books, *Faeries* published by Bantam Books, *Irish Wonders* by D. R. McAnally, Jr., and *Irish Folk and Fairy Tales Omnibus* by Michael Scott.

In mythology swans are the symbol of self-transformation and spiritual liberation. I believe that there is nothing more transforming than loving relationships.

Swan Witch is the second book concerning the romantic adventures of the swan maidens of Myr. The third book, soon to be released, is entitled *Swan Star*.

I would like to hear from my readers. Write:

PO Box 118
Centerville, Utah 84014